The PIRATE BLACKBIRD

BY

UWE TIMM

ILLUSTRATED BY

AXEL SCHEFFLER

TRANSLATED BY NATALIE CURTISS AND JULIE OTTKE

SCHOLASTIC

The PIRATE BLACKBIRD

Published in the UK by Scholastic, 2022
Euston House, 24 Eversholt Street, London, NW1 1DB
Scholastic Ireland, 89E Lagan Road, Dublin Industrial
Estate, Glasnevin, Dublin, D11 HP5F

First published in German under the title *Die Piratenamsel*

ISBN 978 0702 30963 2

A CIP catalogue record for this book is available from the British Library.

Printed by CPI Group (UK) Ltd, Croydon, CR0 4YY
Paper made from wood grown in sustainable
forests and other controlled sources.

1 3 5 7 9 10 8 6 4 2

www.scholastic.co.uk

Chapter 1

Can you guess what kind of bird I am? I bet you can't. No, I'm not a crow… No, I'm not a blackbird… Have you given up yet? All right then, I'll tell you.

I am a myna bird and my name is Froggy. Froggy like a frog or toad. I know, it's a bit of a strange name for a bird. But when I was young and learning to fly, I wasn't

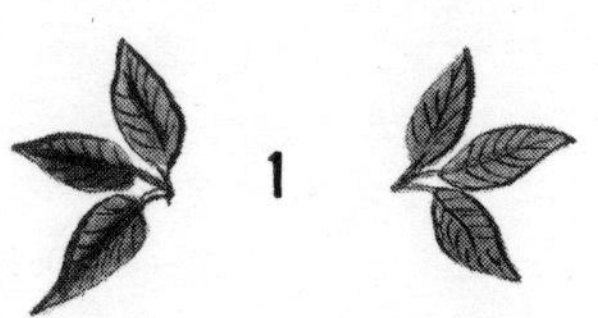

very good at it. I would leap back and forth, trying to fly, like a frog hopping along the ground. My parents decided I was more frog than bird. "We'll call you Froggy," they said.

My parents and I lived in the jungle together. We had LOTS of neighbours, and nearly all of them were colourful. Every other bird was bright and bold, with red, yellow, blue, green, purple or crimson-coloured feathers. They looked as if a rainbow had suddenly grown wings. But not us. We mynas are black as can be, although I do have a very handsome yellow stripe on my head.

As my sister and I perched on our favourite branch, basking in the sunshine, the other

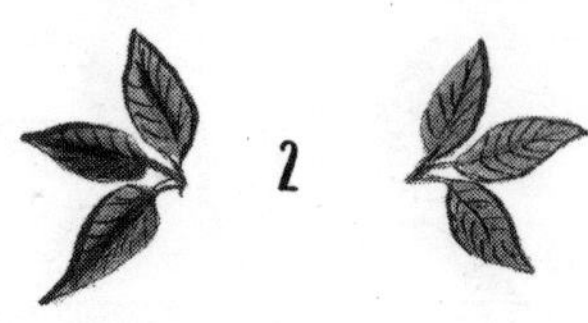

birds would come and tease us, chanting: "Myna, myna – we all look so much finer!"

We'd try to ignore them, but it made us a bit sad. Father would comfort us. One day he said, "It doesn't matter how bright your feathers are, it's all about what you can do!" Then he lowered his voice. "Watch this." He puffed himself up as large as possible, took a deep breath, and suddenly a tiger's growl echoed through the trees.

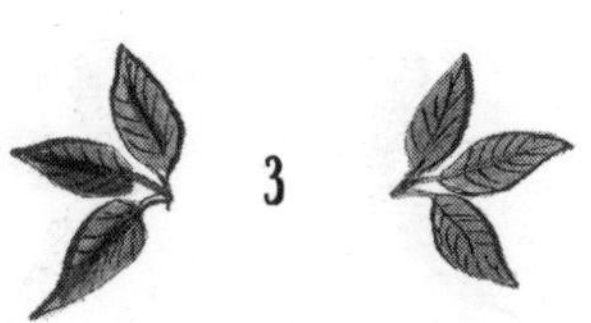

"*ROOOAAARRRR.*"

With a *whoosh* all the colourful birds soared into the sky, squawking loudly, scattering away from the big scary tiger they thought was coming to eat them.

But there was no tiger to be seen. It was my father impersonating one. After a flurry of nervous flapping, the other birds spotted us myna birds with our boring plain feathers sitting together and laughing.

"You silly mynas," the birds shouted, and off they flew.

Father turned to us. "You see? We myna birds might not look like much, but listen to what we can do!"

Mother agreed. "We mynas are perfect at copying any sound. A tiger today, a tortoise

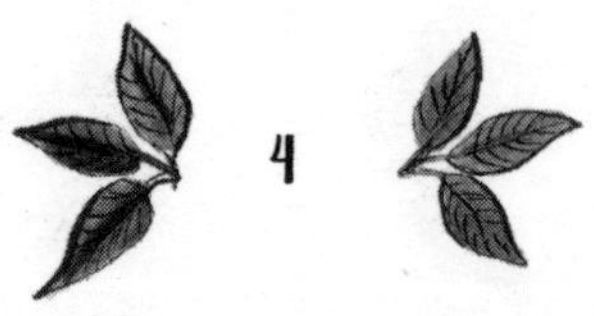

tomorrow. Don't worry, you'll soon learn how to do it."

And so we practised as hard as we could. Every morning we flew with Father to our school branch.

"Listen to me," Father would whisper, and then the most incredible sounds would erupt from him. One moment he was the gurgle of a stream, the next he was chattering like monkeys and rustling like the leaves in the wind.

My sister and I imitated these sounds as well as we could. Father listened and corrected us if the sounds weren't pitch perfect. We had so much fun trying out all the different sounds and we quickly became pretty good.

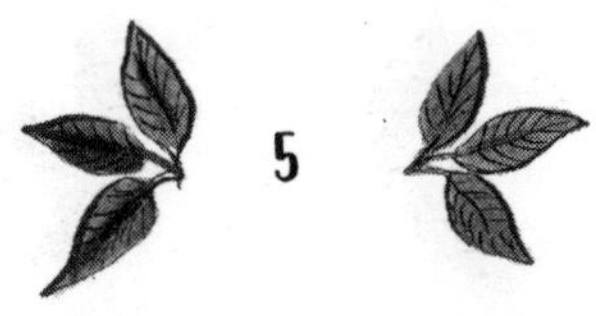

We soon discovered that there was a lot we could do with our new skill. For instance, one of our favourite games became teasing Pandit, the enormous tiger who lived in our jungle. He was very long and very wide – and so large he needed to eat all the time! He crept around ravenously on his massive, silky-soft paws looking for a fat wild boar or a tasty water buffalo to hunt.

One day, I spotted Pandit hunting below me and decided to follow him. *Sniff sniff...* Pandit had sensed a buffalo who was drinking water, unaware of any danger. *Pad, pad, pad...* Pandit snuck up on silent paws and licked his lips with a tongue the size of a towel. Quietly, he approached the buffalo, who was still guzzling down his

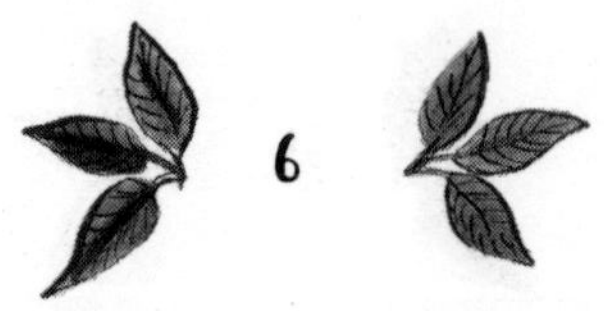

water without a care in the world. Pandit crouched, ready to spring. But at that exact moment, I opened my mouth.

A tiger's roar growled through the trees. The buffalo bolted as fast as his legs could carry him, scampering past Pandit and out of reach.

Pandit howled in rage and searched the thicket, determined to find this other tiger who had so rudely interrupted his hunt. At last, he spotted me high above in the tree – and realized what I'd done. He clawed at the tree trunk with his enormous paws, furiously trying to reach me. He tried to push the tree over and, when that didn't work, he tried to climb it. But the tree was only little, and it bent under his heavy

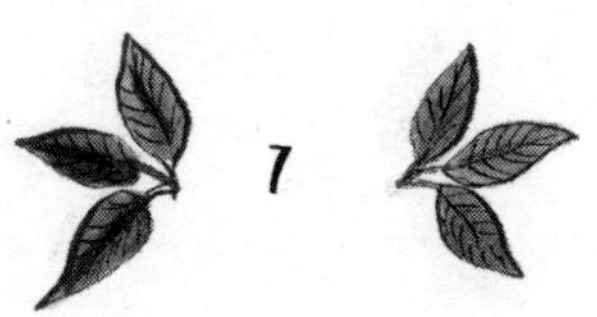

weight – collapsing at last with a *crack* on top of Pandit.

Quickly, I flew away and hid in the undergrowth. But I was having too much fun to stop. I looked out at Pandit from my hiding place and this time I let out a water buffalo's grunt.

Immediately, Pandit leapt up from under the broken tree and tiptoed towards the sound. I grunted again, louder this time. He searched and searched the thicket as I fluttered around, letting out grunts from different places. Finally, I let out one enormous grunt from high above in the treetop where I was sitting. Pandit stared in bewilderment at the branches – how could a water buffalo have flown up into a tree?

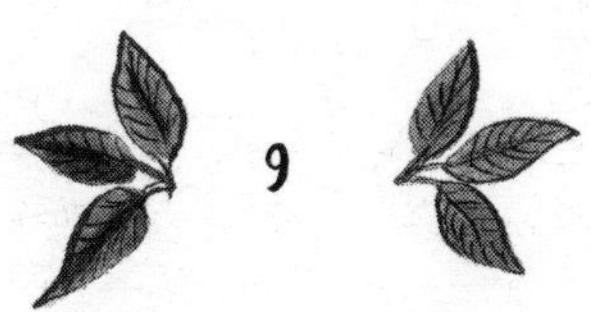

I giggled. "Hello, Pandit, you silly sausage! You may be strong but I'm much cleverer than you." All the other birds in the thicket laughed out loud as Pandit's angry roar shook the trees.

We mynas called this game "Pulling the tiger's tail", but my father always warned us to be careful. "A wise bird does not sit on a rotten branch," he would say sagely.

Chapter 2

Our life in the jungle was perfect. In the mornings we practised making all of the sounds in the jungle, and in the afternoons we played. In the evenings I sat by our hollow and dreamed of the big wide world. Life was good. Until one day I was captured.

That morning we were sitting on our school branch practising, when suddenly a

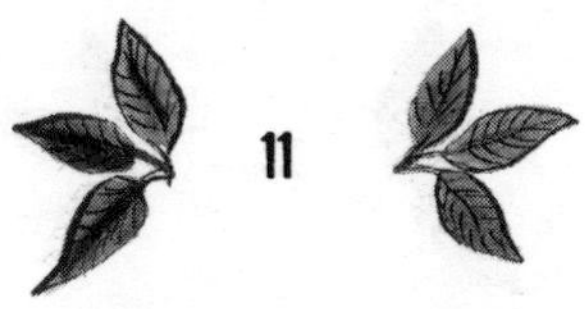

monkey somersaulted across to our tree and shouted, "Careful! There's a man coming!"

My family flew up into the air in a hurry, trying to see what was going on. Not far from my school branch we saw the man. He was spindly thin and on his head was a white hat. The men behind him wore a rolled-up net on their heads.

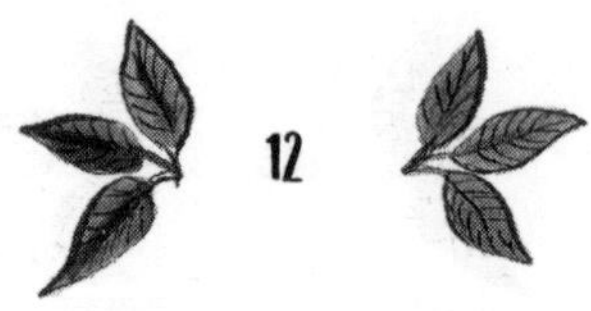

What were they doing here in the jungle with a net? The man pointed to a place by our tree, and the men began to hang the net above the ground – like a big tent.

We mynas sat and watched from a safe distance in the tree. We were all terribly nosy and wondered loudly what was going on. When the net was set up, the man laid fruit and shiny objects inside and disappeared behind a bush.

I couldn't resist flying closer to take a look.

"Be careful," Father hissed.

"Froggy! Stop right there," Mother said.

But it was too late. I had already hopped off the branch on to the ground. I went over to the strange tent. Then, too curious not to investigate, I went inside.

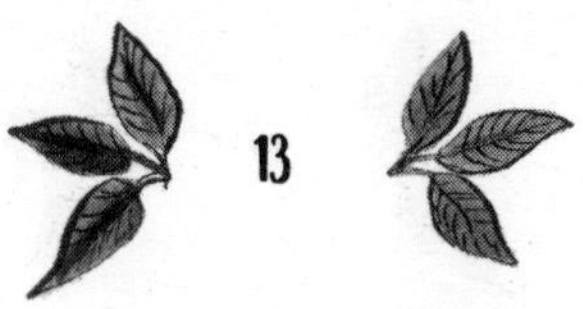

I wasn't the only one. From every tree came all our colourful, nosy neighbours.

We all hopped around the tent, squabbling over the treats inside. Then I spotted something shiny on the ground. It was a mirror. I peered at it, seeing myself for the first time. How handsome I was! As I turned my head this way and that, admiring myself from every angle, I heard a swooshing noise, *RRRUMMSSSHHH*, and the net fell on me and all the other birds.

For a moment I sat there completely dazed. All around me I could feel a terrible fluttering and shouting as the other birds tried to escape. The net was caught tight around us.

The man came and pushed his hand

into the net and, one by one, took us all out. He inspected every single one of us closely. Old or scruffy-feathered birds were let loose to fly away; the others were put in wicker cages.

I cowered in the furthest corner of the net. As the net emptied, the man finally approached me. His hand closed around me, and he pulled me out. He quickly looked me over, and I hoped he would think I was dull compared to the other birds and let me go. But he didn't.

Instead, he put me in a cage like the other birds. A woman took the cage and tied it to the others and carried them off on her head. As she walked away, I took one more look at my lovely old tree where we lived, calling goodbye to my family, before the thick green jungle leaves hid everything from view.

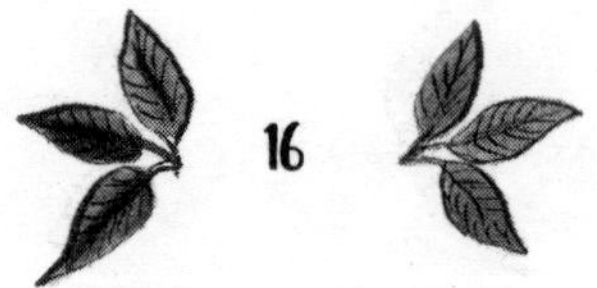

Chapter 3

For three full days the woman carried me through the jungle until we eventually arrived by the sea. We were hauled on to a ship and bundled into a storage room. For a moment I glimpsed the blue sky overhead, then darkness as the hatch was closed. Shortly after, everything began to sway and I could hear the sound of water

rushing outside.

I was cross. “I want to see the world, not be cooped up!” I said. “I can’t see anything in here!”

“Alas,” said a toucan, who had been captured with me. “I’d rather stay at home and skip seeing the world.”

After a long period in the dark, a man appeared at the hatch holding a light in his hand.

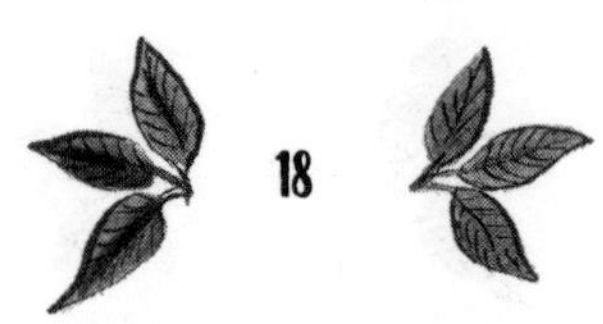

"All right, screechers – time for your grub! My name's Jonny and no one goes hungry on my watch."

He threw some corn and fruit into the cage, muttering all the while, "Here you go, big beak. Nuts for you, nitwit. Apricots for old beady-eye, peaches for the perch hoppers."

I didn't like the way he was speaking to us one little bit. "Big beak!" I called back.

For a moment, Jonny was rooted to the spot. Looking around wildly, he cried, "Where are you hiding, you big mouth?"

"Big mouth!" I called back.

"Show yourself," roared Jonny, "or you'll have me to answer to."

I giggled to myself. Jonny clearly thought

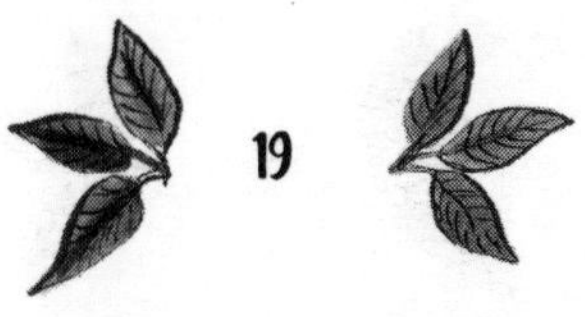

another sailor was teasing him. Jonny blundered about, searching for the culprit, shining his torch into the corners. He bumped his head on a beam in the process. "Ouch!" he shouted.

"Ouch!" I called out, shaking with laughter. My shaking must have given me away for, in that moment, Jonny spotted me. He scratched his head, stared at me, and then burst out laughing.

"Well I never," Jonny said, "a proper chatterbox!"

And with that he brought me to his cabin.

"But keep your beak shut," he said. "It's forbidden to keep animals in the cabins. We'll have to keep you a secret."

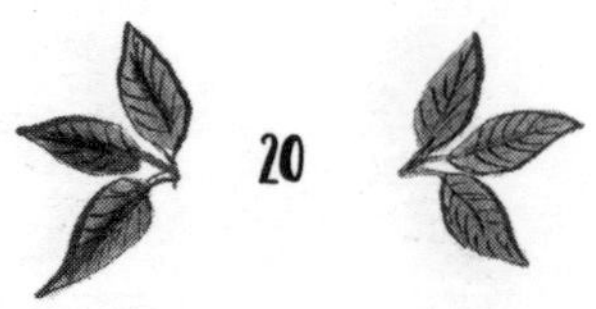

Chapter 4

The cabin was small, but it was cosy, and I was able to see the sea from a little round window which Jonny called a porthole.

The sea was mostly calm; only occasionally did I glimpse small waves with white foam tips splashing at the sides of the ship.

Sometimes, when the ship rocked erratically, Jonny would pull out a bottle of

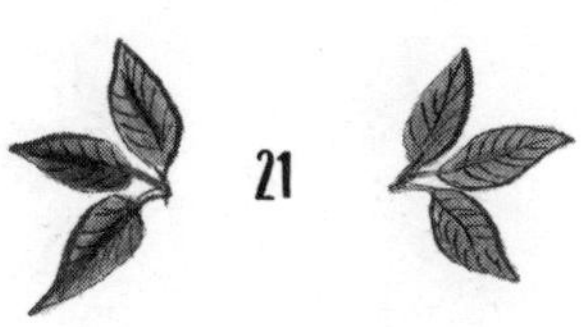

his special banana drink. One day he offered me a sip. "Helps against sea sickness," he said.

I tried it cautiously. It was incredibly sweet and so sticky it nearly stuck my beak together!

"Someone's been stealing it," said Jonny, carefully putting the bottle away. "I can tell."

During the day, Jonny would steer the ship or beat the rust from the ship's hull. This was an important job as a build-up of rust could cause ships to sink.

In the evenings, Jonny would light his pipe and settle down for a rest, flexing his left arm muscle, which made his seagull tattoo look as if it was flapping its wings. "How about I teach you proper sailor

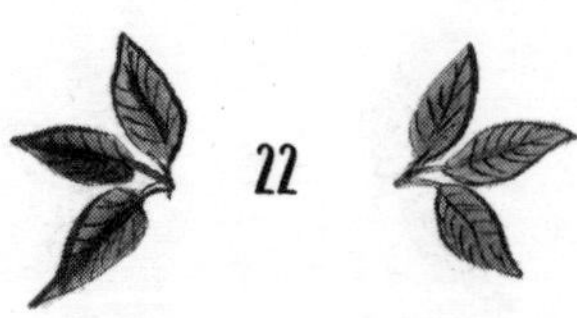

lingo?" he said one evening – and so began a strange new school.

"Hello, captain, you ol' perch hopper," he would say.

"Hello, captain, you ol' perch hopper," I would say back, and he would double up with laughter.

I slept during the day as Jonny's loud snoring made my cage vibrate too much to get any rest at night. One morning, I imitated Jonny's snoring. He gasped and said, "Shiver me timbers! That's a pretty scary tiger impression."

One night I was wide awake as usual when I heard a scratching sound against the door. Slowly, the door opened and a figure tiptoed into the cabin. They leaned over Jonny,

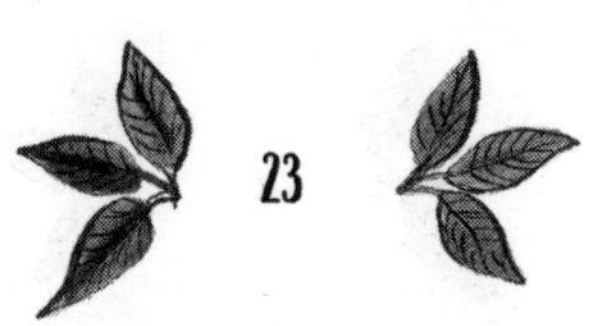

who was snoring loudly and contentedly. Reassured, the figure snuck up to the cupboard, opened it quietly and started to rummage inside. This must be the thief who was stealing Jonny's special drink! I let out a roar just like the one I had used to scare the buffalo away from the tiger, Pandit. The figure dropped the bottle with a crash and ran out of the door as fast as they could.

Jonny sat bolt upright in bed. "Shiver me timbers," he said, rubbing his sleepy eyes. "What a dream ... I thought I was in the jungle and a scurvy tiger got me pants. Enormous set of teeth he had too!"

The next morning, a high-ranking officer walked into Jonny's cabin, his three

golden stripes glistening on his sleeve.

"I've heard reports that you have a wild animal in here. Have you been hiding a tiger?" he asked Jonny, looking doubtfully around the cabin.

"Nah," Jonny replied, "he'd be a little big for this cabin."

"What's the crow doing here?" the officer asked, spotting me.

"Big mouth!" I cried.

"What did you say?" said the officer indignantly, staring at Jonny.

"Wasn't me," Jonny said. "It was the bird."

"Put him back in the cargo hold immediately," bellowed the officer, and slammed the door shut behind him as he marched out.

"Oh well," Jonny said. "I guess you need to go back with the others. Not to worry, though, it won't be for long. In two days' time we'll be arriving in London."

Chapter 5

Jonny was right. After two days of darkness in the hold, the rocking motion stopped. The hatch above the storage room was lifted and a large hook swayed downwards.

Our cage was hung on to the hook and we were lifted off the ship and high into the sky. We hung there for a long time, still caged but out in the open and the fresh

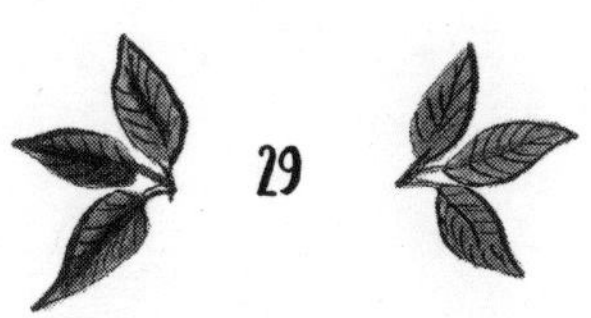

air. The sun shone and the wind blew our feathers. I saw Jonny down below – he waved at me and called out, "Take care and keep your chin up, chatterbox!"

The cage was slowly lowered until we bumped on to dry land where men carried our cages to a van. Doors were slammed and, once again, we sat in darkness.

"Doesn't this ever end?" moaned the toucan. "I'm fed up of being in darkness, squished into a small cage. If only I could stretch out my beak and wings."

Before long, the van door was wrenched open and we were carried into a large room. There were animals *everywhere*: birds, fish, dogs, cats, water fleas, guinea pigs, golden hamsters and small reptiles.

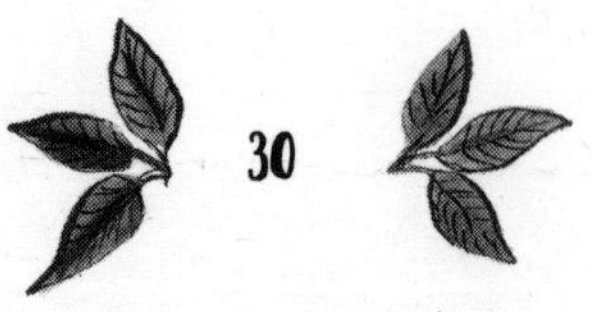

Aha, I thought. *This must be a pet shop.*

A bald-headed man with enormous, hairy ears took me out of the cage and sprinkled me with a powder that stank.

"Don't want any fleas hopping around," he said as he rubbed it in.

After this unwelcome treatment, he brought me over to a large cage in the window. There were two other cages there as well. In the largest cage was an old parrot, and in the other was a cockatoo who turned to look me up and down.

The cockatoo squawked, "How d'you do, how d'you do?" before returning to preening his feathers proudly. I had to admit they were beautifully white and shone in the sun. He paused only to

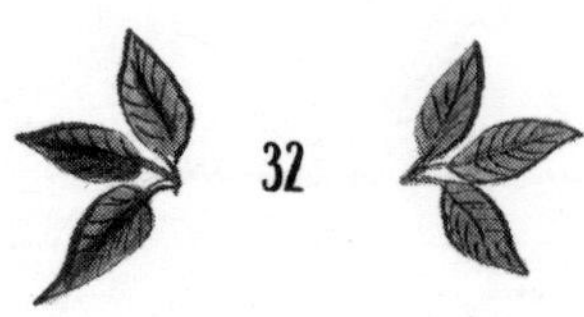

remark, "Look what the cat dragged in. A common crow, making itself at home in the spotlight."

"How rude," I replied. "I'm not the one showing off."

"You're jealous," cried the cockatoo. "You just want to have beautiful shiny feathers like me."

He puffed out his chest and strutted up and down on his perch. "How d'you do, how d'you do?" he called to the people passing by. Children on their way home from school pressed their noses flat against the glass of the window.

"You're right," said the old parrot to me. "That cockatoo is a real show-off. Don't worry about him, little fella. I'll look out

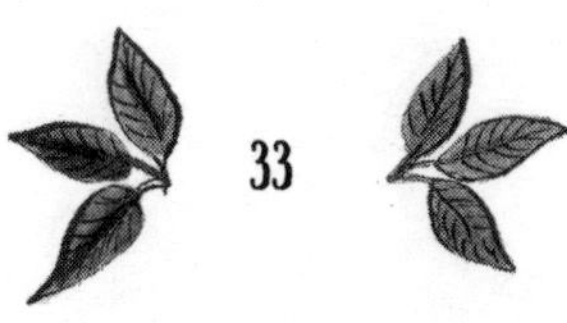

for you. My name is Blackbeard, and I've sailed the Seven Seas."

"I'm Froggy," I replied softly.

"And where do you come from?" the parrot asked kindly.

"India," I said, and suddenly burst into tears.

"There, there..." said Blackbeard sympathetically. "When your heart is heavy a good cry works wonders. But just you wait and see – it's not so bad in England, I promise. A little cold, maybe, but you can have a good life here."

Chapter 6

I soon got used to life in the pet shop. There was a constant stream of customers, but no one seemed very interested in the birds in the window. Most people who visited the pet shop bought fish or hamsters or rats.

The man who ran the pet shop was called Mr Lyon. He would stop each customer and ask them if they would like to buy a talking

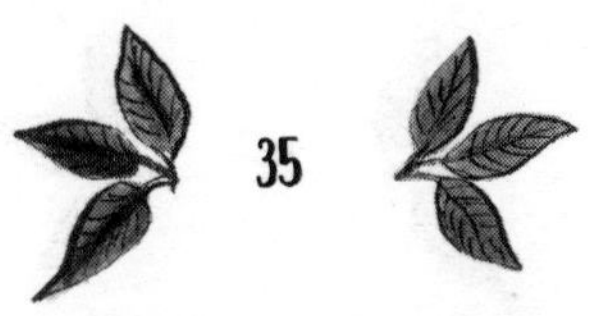

bird. They all exclaimed in wonder over the lovely cockatoo but when they heard the price Mr Lyon named, they went pale and said "no, thank you" rather quickly. He was too expensive. And no one seemed interested in me or old Blackbeard.

Only once did someone want me. It was a little girl who was with her mother. They had come in to buy food for her guinea pigs but then the little girl spotted me and tugged at her mother's arm.

"Look at that bird; isn't he lovely?" said the little girl.

"He's called a cockatoo," said her mother, who was in the middle of paying.

"No," said the little girl, "I mean that one." She pointed at me.

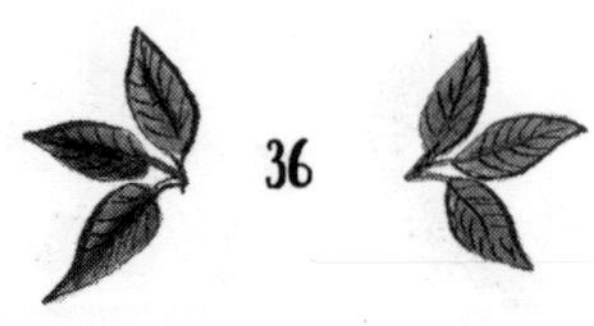

"The crow?" said the mum, swinging round to stare at me.

"That isn't a crow. It has a yellow stripe on its head. It's a pirate blackbird!" the girl said excitedly.

"Nonsense!" Her mother laughed. "Pirate blackbirds don't exist. It's definitely a crow."

"Oh, can't we buy him, PLEASE?" begged the girl.

"That's all we need! You already have two guinea pigs and now you want a crow."

"Did you know," said Blackbeard, "I think grown-ups should really be called grown-uppities? They always seem to know better. Let me tell you a story and you'll see what I mean. I once knew a wolf who came from Siberia, far away from here. He walked

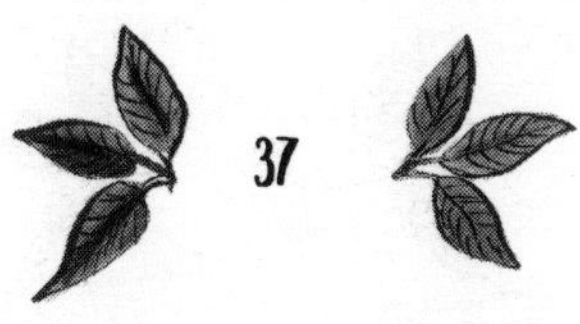

and walked until he reached a London park. He thought everyone would be pleased to see a real wolf as wolves don't live here any more. As he sat in the town park, he gobbled down some bread that people had thrown for the ducks when a father and his son walked by.

'Look there, Dad,' said the boy, 'there's a wolf eating bread.'

'Rubbish,' replied the father, 'that isn't a wolf. That's a dog. A German shepherd dog, to be exact.'

'No, that's a wolf,' said the boy.

'How on earth could a wolf have got into a London park? There are no wolves in England! It's a dog.'

'No, that's a wolf without a doubt.'

'You do have a vivid imagination,' laughed the father, and patted the wolf. 'See?' the father said. 'It's just an ordinary German shepherd.'

The wolf was so sad to hear this, he walked the long journey back to Siberia."

I didn't know what to say after Blackbeard had told his story, so I just sat there silently, watching the girl and her mother leave the shop.

Chapter 7

Life in the pet shop was quite pleasant. We birds all sat in the display window and chatted together, waiting for new customers. One afternoon, an elegant older lady entered the shop. Mr Lyon approached her, rubbing his hands together.

For once, Mr Lyon was in luck – the lady wanted to buy a talking bird. Mr Lyon's

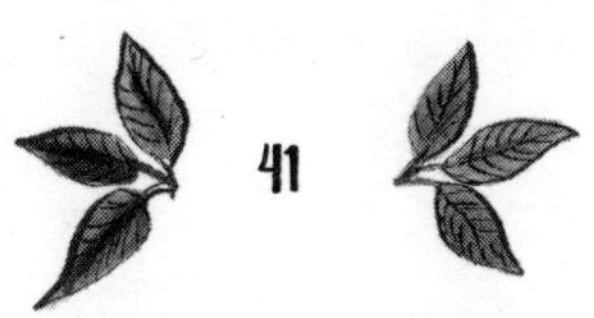

huge ears glowed red with excitement. He led the lady over to us.

"Here are *three* talking birds," he announced grandly.

The cockatoo strutted on the perch and said coyly, "How d'you do, how d'you do?" He peeked up at the lady from beneath his feathers.

"I like chocolate," said the old lady. "Say: I like chocolate," she demanded.

The silly little cockatoo didn't understand. "How d'you do?" babbled the cockatoo. "How d'you do?"

"Can't he say anything else except 'how d'you do'?" the lady said coldly.

"He's a beautiful bird," answered Mr Lyon hastily, as the hair on his ears bristled.

"Just look at the wonderful colour of his feathers."

"Yes, yes," replied the lady, "but I want a bird that can say a little more than just 'how d'you do'. The bird has to amuse my guests at my coffee mornings. What about that one over there…?" She pointed at Blackbeard, looking down her nose at his scruffy feathers. "He looks rather sullen. Are you sure he can talk?"

"That's a parrot, madam. He belonged to an old sailor and knows all the sailing commands. Say 'batten down the hatches', Blackbeard."

Blackbeard eyed the rude old lady beadily. He didn't open his beak. The lady walked closer to Blackbeard's cage, bringing her

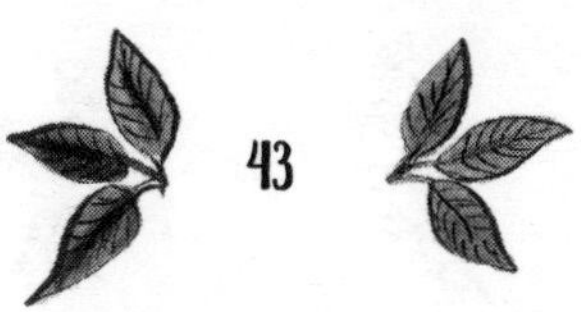

face right up to his, and once again said, "I like chocolate, I like chocolate" in a sing-song voice.

Blackbeard stared back and let out a croak like a hooded crow. "*KRAHH KRAAH KRAHH.*"

The lady jumped back in fright. "Goodness," she said, pursing her lips. "What a funny, grouchy thing."

At that, Blackbeard splatted a white runny poo straight on to her fine dress.

"Argh," cried the lady. "What a horrid beast. And my dress, just look at my dress – it's ruined. You'll have to pay for it to be cleaned."

"Please accept my apologies," begged Mr Lyon, and his ears turned quite white

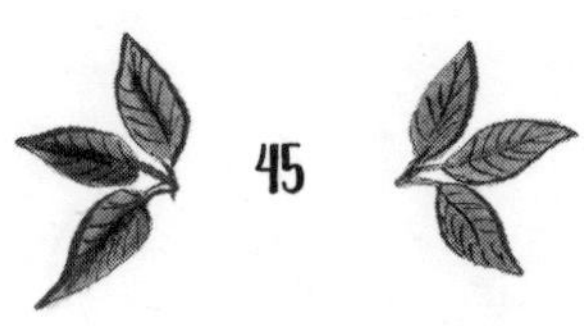

instead of their usual red. "I'm so sorry, my dear lady. And your dress will be fine – in my experience if you dry it the poo will simply brush off..."

But the lady had already turned to look at me, the last bird of the bunch. "What an ugly-looking thing," she said. "A crow, isn't it?"

"No," said Mr Lyon. "It's a myna bird. The myna bird may not *look* spectacular, but of all the birds they are the best talkers. Better than parrots."

"Interesting," said the lady, sounding anything but interested.

"Interesting," I said, wanting to show her that I was more than a silly crow.

"Ah." The lady laughed. "Just listen – how wonderful."

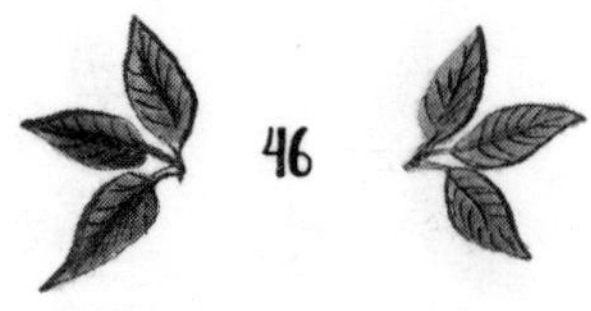

"Ah," I said in her voice. "Just listen – how wonderful."

Pursing her lips again she said, "Sweeeet chocolate, say: sweeeet chocolate."

"Sweeeeet chocolate," I said. "Big mouth. Screecher."

"Well!" the lady said to Mr Lyon. "How rude! Thank you and good day. You can stick your bird under your hat."

And with that she marched out of the shop.

Blackbeard laughed and called out to her retreating back, "Thank you and good day! You can stick your bird under your hat."

Mr Lyon approached Blackbeard, his ears redder than I'd ever seen them before.

"I'm not stupid!" he yelled. "You can talk

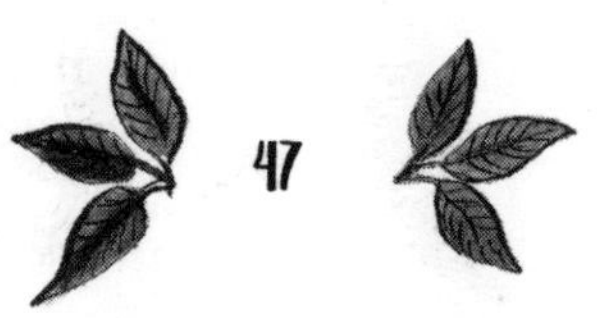

very well when you want to! But you *don't* want to. All you do is sit around and stare and eat. Watch out, I am going to sell you some day. I'll persuade *someone* to buy you, mark my words."

Chapter 8

"That was a close call," Blackbeard whispered. "Just be careful; that lady almost bought you. You would have sat in her front room repeating 'I like chocolate' day in and day out. What a terrible life."

"You think so?" I asked.

"Trust me," Blackbeard said. "I've seen it all." And he began to tell me his life story.

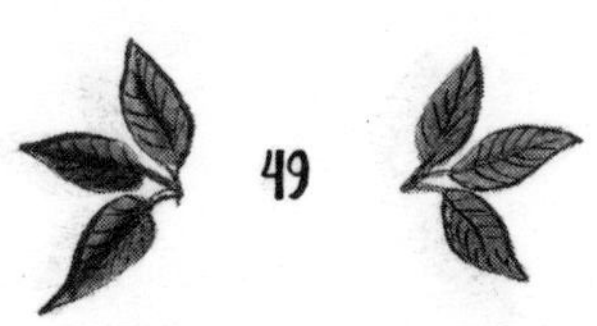

"I was born one hundred and forty years ago on an island not far from the equator. One day, a raging storm hit the island and blew me from my nest. I was found by a sailor named Charlie. Those were the good old days," said Blackbeard wistfully. "The ship we sailed on – it was an island of white sails in the middle of the sea, not like those steamboats which mess up your feathers with soot or those motor boats which stink of diesel oil. On a sailing ship you can fly from mast to mast and yard to yard. Like a swimming forest! And the sailors would sing their sea shanty:

'When the sea is choppy and grey
And night hardly changes to day

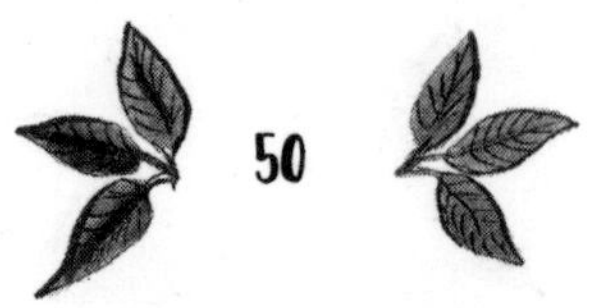

I look to the sky with my sailor's eye
To guide us the safe and right way.'"

Blackbeard's eyes welled up. "Charlie was a fine fellow who always gave me plenty of food and a little sip from his cask. Once, I even danced on the waves."

"What? That's impossible," I said.

"No, it's very much possible. When a hurricane hit and our ship started to sink, Charlie told me to jump into the water. But I couldn't swim. So, Charlie chucked the empty cask overboard and jumped in after me. He held on to some floating timber while I perched on the casket, bobbing up and down on the waves. It was really hard to stay on the cask. 'Run!' shouted Charlie.

So I ran on the waves. I had never run as much in my entire life."

"Why didn't you fly instead?" I asked.

"Boy, you have no clue about hurricanes, do you? I would have been swept away in five minutes."

"What happened then?" I asked.

"Well, a day later the wind died down and another sailing boat appeared. Charlie cried for help, but they were too far away. 'Go, Blackbeard, fly up high,' he told me. When they spotted me, they knew immediately that a ship had sunk as parrots don't fly over the sea. They pulled us out of the water. A fine chap, Charlie was," he said pensively.

"And where is Charlie now?"

"Charlie was promoted through the

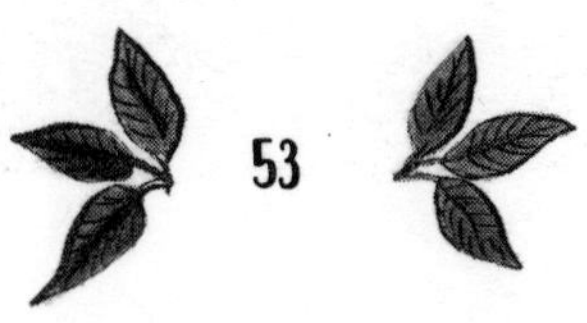

seafarer ranks. We sailed the fastest ships and often found ourselves in great danger. It was quite the life."

"And what happened next?" I asked.

"When Charlie reached a ripe old age, he moved us into an old seafarer's home down by the River Thames. From there we could see all the ships on the river. Just picture it, loads of old sailors pulling each other's legs."

"Pulling each other's legs!" I said. "That must have been painful."

"No, no," said Blackbeard. "It's an expression – it means they were telling each other tall tales. Fibs! They would describe their adventures at sea: waves as high as mountains, colossal whales, wind breaking on the shore."

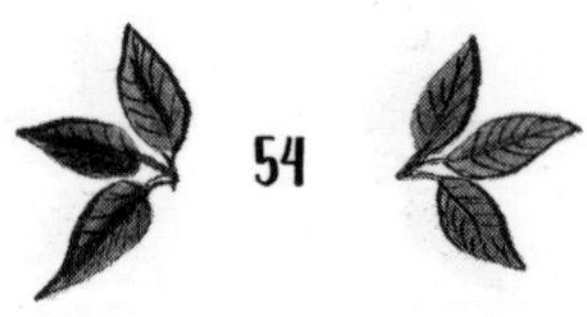

How strange, I thought. *I always thought breaking wind meant farting!* But I didn't say anything.

"And then Charlie died," said Blackbeard. He stared into space. "It was terrible. I was sold to a fridge salesman called Mr Dovetail. I don't particularly like doves, you know. The guy was always away on business selling his fridges. For days I was left alone in the flat, bored to death, and when he was at home he would plonk himself on the couch and stare at the TV.

"Eventually, Mr Dovetail gave me away to his beast of a nephew. The little boy always taunted me – he would try and pull out my tail feathers, poured glue over me and put ink in my water bowl. After that, his mother sold

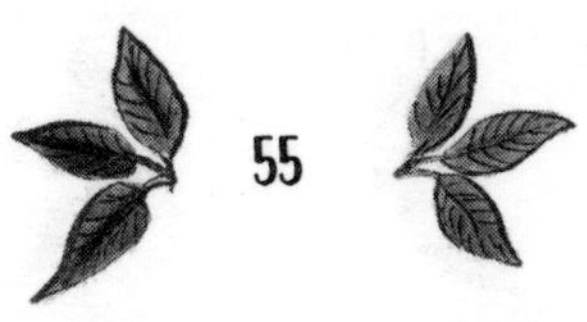

me to this pet shop. And here I am. It's not a bad life here with old Jug-Ears. There are lots of animals to chat to and the kids enjoy watching us from outside the shop window. We all have a roof over our heads and enough food – what else could one wish for? Just be careful not to get sold one day. You never know where you might end up."

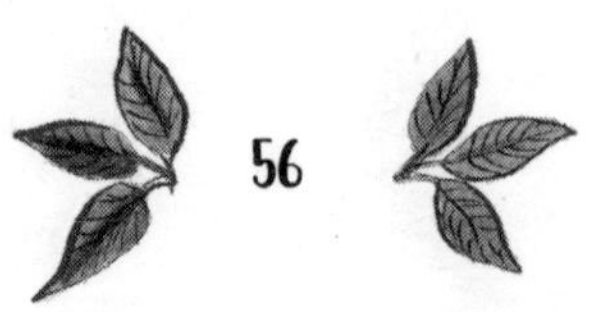

Chapter 9

One day the cockatoo was sold. Jug-Ears, the name that Blackbeard had given Mr Lyon, had managed to persuade an old lady to buy him.

The cockatoo was over the moon, proud that someone had bought him. He told us all that he was going to sit in a golden cage. "How d'you do, how d'you do?" he

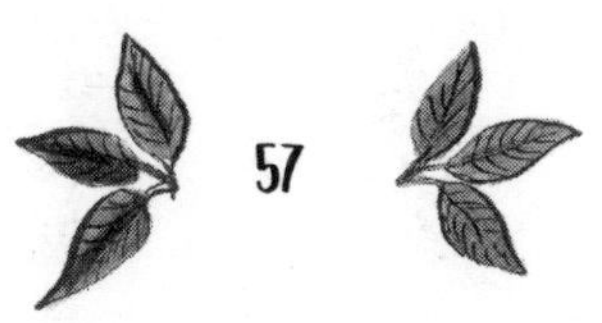

called in glee.

Then, something terrible happened.

The old lady poked her index finger into the cage to stroke the cockatoo's head. Overcome with excitement, he bit her finger.

"That bird bites!" screamed the lady. Outraged, she held her bloody finger under Mr Lyon's nose. "I want my money back!"

Mr Lyon gave the lady her money back and she left the shop. Then he turned to us and roared: "That's enough, you three vultures! One of you is stupid, the next stubborn and the third is rude. I've reached the end of my tether."

"What's his tether?" asked the cockatoo, distraught. "I didn't mean for that to

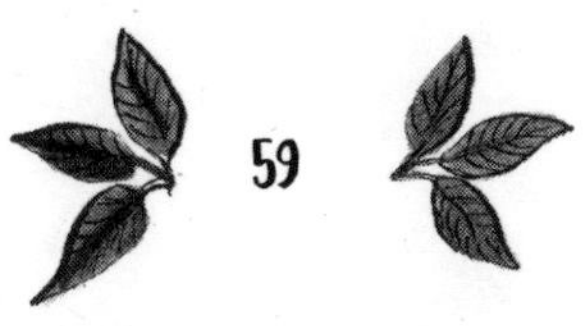

happen, I just wanted to give her a little peck to show how happy I was."

"Keep your beak shut," said Blackbeard warningly.

"Why are you telling me off?" asked the cockatoo.

"You three birds just sit there! Doing nothing!" roared Mr Lyon, and his bald head glowed dark crimson. "I want you out of my hair."

"How do we get out of his hair?" asked the cockatoo. "He doesn't have any!"

Blackbeard sighed. "He's saying that he wants to earn some money from us. He bought us and wants to sell us for a profit. You must understand that this is a pet shop and not a zoo."

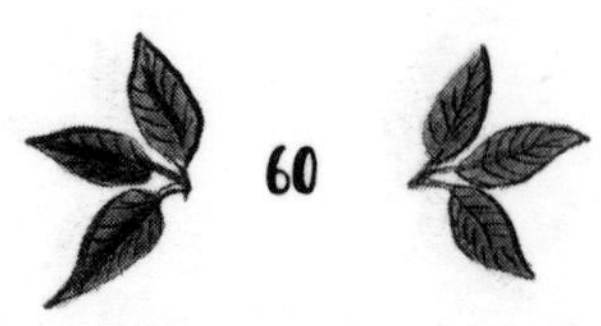

"Will he let us fly away?" I asked.

"No," said the cockatoo defiantly. "I'm going to stay in my cage. One day I shall live in a big house in a snow-white cage like I deserve."

As we'd been talking, Jug-Ears had stomped over to the telephone and made a call. His gaze turned to us as he laid down the telephone receiver and said, "Now you'll do something useful." He grinned deviously.

"He's going to kill us," wailed the cockatoo.

"Rubbish," said Blackbeard.

"I don't know about you, but I'm sure I'm a delicacy," said the cockatoo anxiously.

We sat and waited. I was nervous

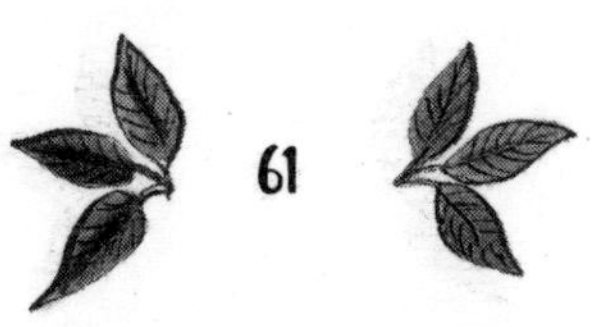

and Blackbeard cleared his throat again and again.

Late that afternoon, two men in uniform entered the shop.

"Are they police officers?" I asked. "Are we going to prison?"

"Calm down," said Blackbeard.

Jug-Ears pointed at us. "That's them."

One man grabbed both Blackbeard's cage and mine; the other man took the large cage where the cockatoo crouched.

The cockatoo shouted excitedly, "How d'you do, how d'you do?" He was delighted to have been bought, even though we had no idea where we were going.

We were carried to a delivery van and behind us someone slammed the door shut.

It was completely dark. At every turn we clung on for dear life so that we wouldn't be squashed against the cage bars.

"Splendid," babbled the cockatoo. "Bought at last! They will surely put me into a lovely big room with large windows and valuable furniture, and when visitors come to the house I will amuse them."

"If you don't immediately shut your beak," snapped Blackbeard, "I'll tell them it's been a mistake and that you're just an ordinary chicken and then you'll end up in the oven."

The cockatoo fell silent and for a while there was nothing but the grumble of traffic and the occasional cough from Blackbeard.

Suddenly, the van stopped. In the distance I heard the familiar sound of a tiger roaring.

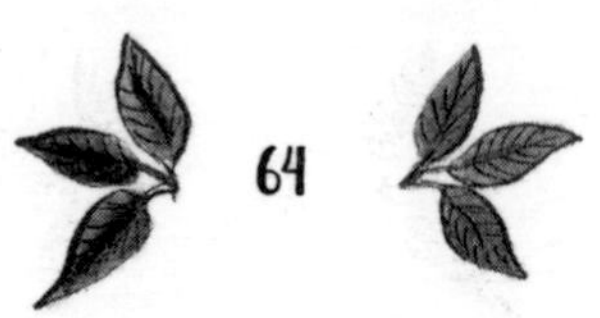

"Hooray," I shouted excitedly, "we're back in India."

"Impossible," mumbled Blackbeard. "You don't get to India that quickly by car."

The tiger roared again.

"That's odd," said Blackbeard.

Then the door was wrenched open. In front of us, we could see a rock on which monkeys were climbing around.

"Africa," shouted the cockatoo.

"Nope. Colchester Zoo," said Blackbeard.

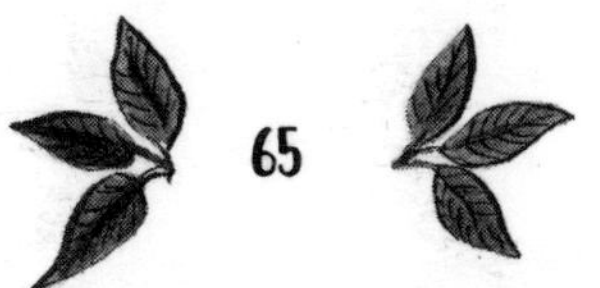

Chapter 10

Mr Lyon had sold us to the zoo – way below our market price.

"This is great," I said. "Look! There are elephants walking around!"

We were carried to a man dressed in white overalls.

"A vet," whispered Blackbeard. "Watch out, he'll jab you with a needle. They call

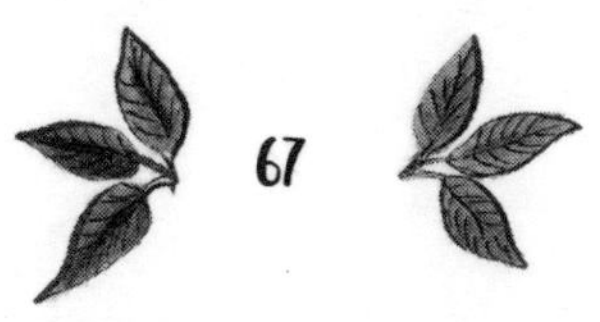

it a vaccination."

All three of us were vaccinated. Ouch.

"That's already the sixth time in my life," moaned Blackbeard.

Afterwards, a keeper carried us to a large birdcage. For the first time in months, I could fly a little. Not very far, but I could finally stretch my wings after being cooped

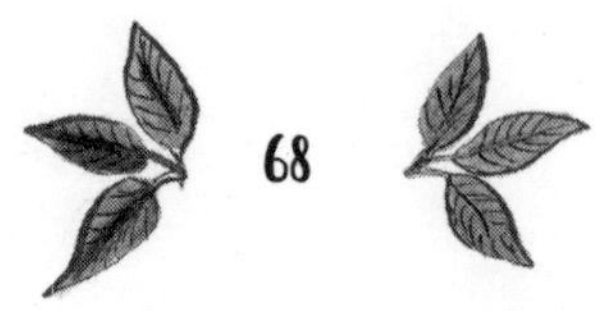

up in a cage. The cockatoo sat on a branch near to the wire mesh of the cage where some visitors stood, walking haughtily up and down saying "How d'you do, how d'you do?"

Blackbeard had found a bare tree in the far corner of the cage.

"Quite nice here," said Blackbeard. "You can sit in the open and let the wind blow around your beak. But the company is … terrible."

He was right. It wasn't just us three any more. With us in the cage were hundreds of birds flapping around. They sang, twittered, chirped and cooed all together. The cacophony was almost like being at home in the jungle. And again, just like

at home, all the other birds were bright and colourful. I had just completed a few rounds in the cage, surveying my new home, when along came a bird of paradise.

He took one look at me and shouted, "Just look at that, they've put a common crow into the cage! Boring!"

"Maybe he's not really a crow," said another bird of paradise. "He's got a yellow stripe on his head." She hopped a bit closer. "Maybe he's a yellow bird in disguise. Let's take a look."

The bird began to pluck at my feathers. It was the final straw. I opened my beak and I growled like the tiger Pandit: "*GRRRRRRRR.*"

WHOOSH! The birds scattered around

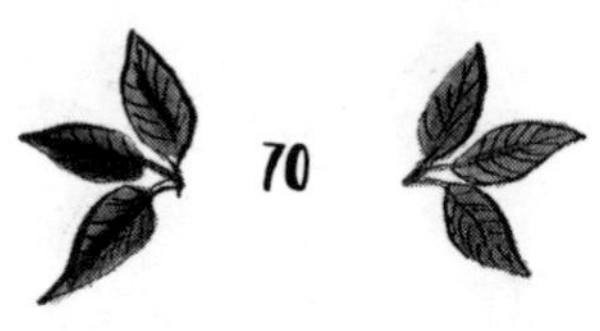

and settled in fright on the top branches of the trees.

In the next cage a tiger answered my growl with a rather tired and half-hearted roar.

Chapter 11

I was far better suited to zoo life than life in a pet shop. I could fly around, for one thing. The food, however, was awful. It was a terrible medley of seeds, mashed-up fruits, all blended up with vitamin powders. It was supposed to be a balanced diet that would keep all bird species happy – but it failed to please a single one of us. It was disgusting.

The bird keeper who looked after us was called Oscar and he knew each and every one of us by name. During the opening hours, the visitors would crowd around the cages and stare at us – or rather, they would stare at all the other birds. I was so dull and boring that no one looked at me.

Only once did someone pay me any attention.

"Look, over there, it's the pirate blackbird!" I heard a voice cry.

I recognized the voice right away. It was the little girl I had encountered in Mr Lyon's pet shop. Her mother tried to pull her away, saying, "Come on, let's move on to the rhinos and let the old crow be."

"It's not a crow," she replied firmly, licking

her ice cream. "It is a pirate blackbird."

"Nonsense!" And, with that, the mother pulled the girl away into the bustling crowd of weekend zoo visitors.

After a few weeks I had thoroughly explored my cage, had sat on every branch in sight and had flown into every corner. With nothing else to do, I resorted to my old tricks.

The two birds of paradise, who I had found out were called William and Matilda, were easily tricked. It was fun teasing them. They were the celebrities of our birdcage due to their beautiful plumage. They were both pretty full of themselves thanks to the constant praise and adoration from the zoo visitors. The cockatoo, whom I had

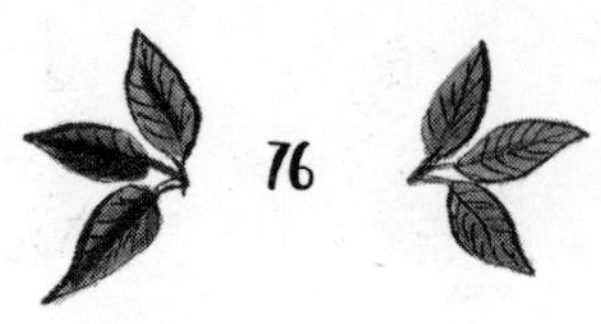

once thought pompous and arrogant, now seemed rather humble in comparison.

Every day, Matilda sat in one cage corner, William in the other, each intent on drawing the biggest crowd. One day, I made sure I was hidden in the middle of the cage and mimicked William's voice.

"Hello, Matilda, you common swan."

"How dare you call me a common swan, William!" Matilda squawked. "You old swamp thrush."

"Excuse me," crowed William, showing his blue iridescent tail feathers. "Me? A swamp thrush? You boring quail."

"You silly bird," screeched Matilda.

"Hooded crow," bellowed William.

That was clearly the last straw. They

charged at each other and feathers flew into the air as they fought. I watched, giggling.

"Will you give over, you hoodlums." Oscar the zoo keeper arrived on the scene and separated the squabbling birds. He picked up William's beautiful tail feather which Matilda had plucked out and said,

"Instead of tearing out each other's feathers you should be laying some eggs."

But, despite having looked after the birds for years, Oscar didn't know everything. Matilda wasn't going to be laying eggs any time soon. She was a boy.

Chapter 12

After three weeks in the zoo, I couldn't stop myself staring up at the swallows in the sky through the wire mesh of the cage. How wonderful it must be to fly with them.

One day I flew to Blackbeard and said, "I want to escape."

"Why?" he asked. "It's really quite cosy here. You can get used to the food."

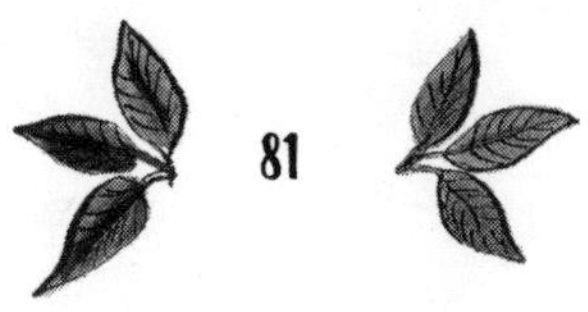

"No," I said. "I don't like just sitting around in a cage. Now that I'm here in England, I want to explore. I don't want to be caged with the same birds I could see back home in the jungle. I've got to get out of here."

Blackbeard tilted his head. "That won't be easy, my dear. In zoos they lock animals in so they can't escape." He looked around thoughtfully. "Why don't you talk to the hummingbird? He's been here a long time. In fact, he was born in a cage."

I flew over to the hummingbird.

"You want to leave here?" said the hummingbird. "Forget it. Never going to happen. No bird has ever escaped. Besides, why bother? We have everything we could

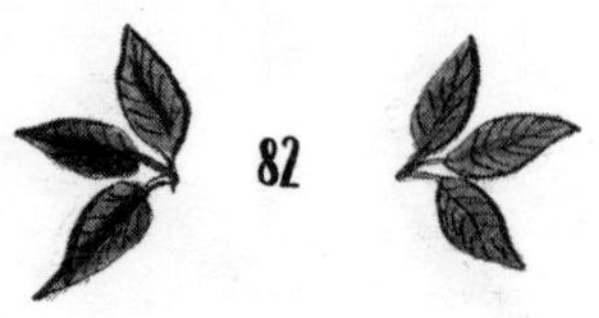

ever want here."

"I'll manage," I said.

"We'll see about that," answered the hummingbird.

I perched in my tree and thought hard about how I might escape. I did that for three days. Every day Oscar the bird keeper would ask me, "What's the matter with you, then?"

I didn't reply. I was too busy thinking.

On the third day he brought me to the vet and said, "This bird refuses to eat. Is he ill?"

The vet examined me closely. "Maybe he has a cold, or he could be homesick – try giving him his favourite food."

The next morning Oscar brought me a mango. But I was too busy thinking to

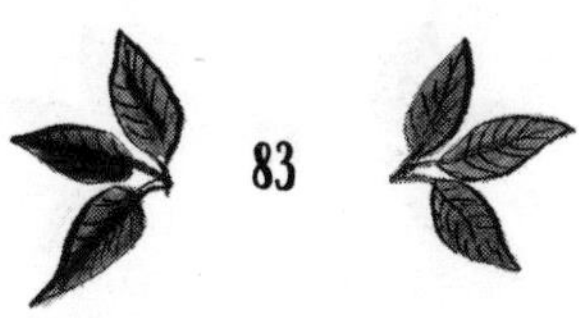

be hungry.

Oscar shook his head and scattered the bird seed into different dishes. At that moment, his friend the tiger keeper came over and quietly stood behind Oscar and shouted, “Beware! The tiger has escaped!”

Oscar took no notice as the tiger keeper made the same joke every day.

“Stop talking rubbish,” he said. “When the tiger really does escape no one will believe you.”

The tiger keeper laughed and said: “If the tiger did escape then you wouldn’t get any warning, you would just hear a roaring growl behind you.”

Then an idea came into my head. A plan that would free me from my cage. I flew

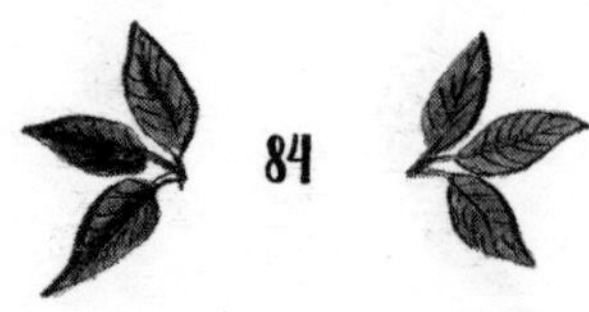

over to Blackbeard, told him about my plan and asked if he wanted to come with me.

"Oh, no," said Blackbeard. "I feel quite at home here. Flying is getting harder for me. I'm no longer a spring chicken, you know. It's not so bad sitting here and watching the people. Look at that tall man in the raincoat – he looks like a crow. And that woman with the bird feed – she's got so much hair the ostriches could nest in it."

"I don't like being stared at all day," I said.

"Why not?" laughed Blackbeard. "It doesn't hurt us." Blackbeard wished me luck and said, "If you need help out there, send word and I will come. Chin up, sails high, sailor."

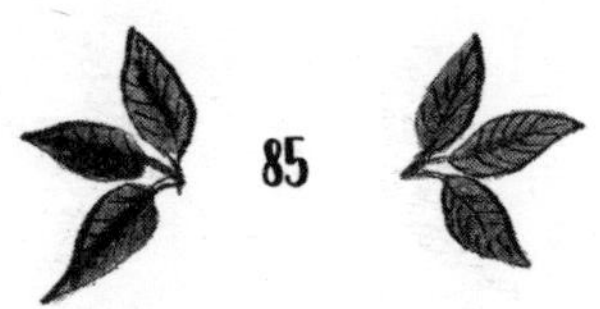

Chapter 13

The time came to enact my escape plan.

The first thing I did was have a hearty breakfast. In the afternoon Oscar saw that I had eaten the mango fruit and said, "Wonderful! Our little myna bird is feeling better."

He scattered the feed into a large dish and as he did, I flew right behind him, took a

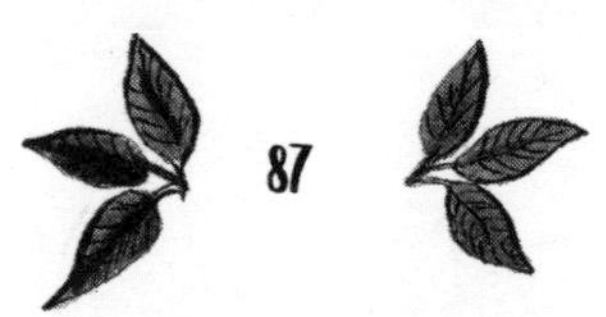

deep breath, and roared just like the tiger Pandit. *GRRRRRRR*.

Then, in the tiger keeper's voice, I cried, "Help, the tiger has escaped!"

Poor old Oscar. He leapt up in shock, dropped the feeding dish, ran to the nearest

building and locked the door behind him. It happened to be a toilet.

Of course, in his haste he didn't lock the cage door. The visitors who would stand and stare at us in our cages also fled. They hid in dustbins, climbed trees and crawled on top of the bird house. I growled once more and this time the caged tiger nearby growled too – louder than he ever had before. *GRRRRRRR*.

In the birdcage there was total chaos. All the birds fluttered in fear – Matilda even lost some tail feathers in the excitement. The cockatoo walked up and down a branch calling, "How d'you do, how d'you do?" thinking all the fuss was for him.

Only Blackbeard sat calmly on his bare

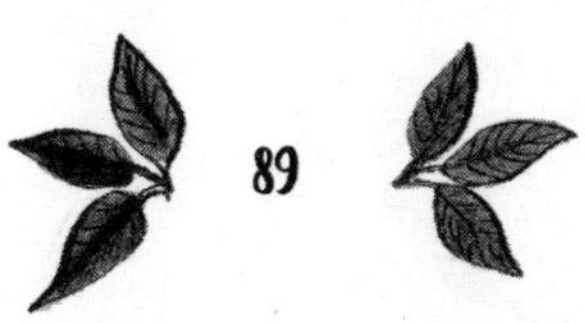

tree and laughed.

I called out, "The cage is open! You can all fly to wherever you want." But not one other bird wanted to leave.

"Rather not," said the hummingbird. "Soon it will be winter and then it will be very cold."

I flew to Blackbeard and called, "Oh, please, come with me, Blackbeard."

"No, thanks. Sorry," he answered. "But I wish you all the best."

I flew out of the cage – my heart lifting at last now that I was free. What a wonderful feeling it was to soar in the air, with only clouds and sky above me. Finally no net, no cage to stop me.

Beneath me, looking quite small, I

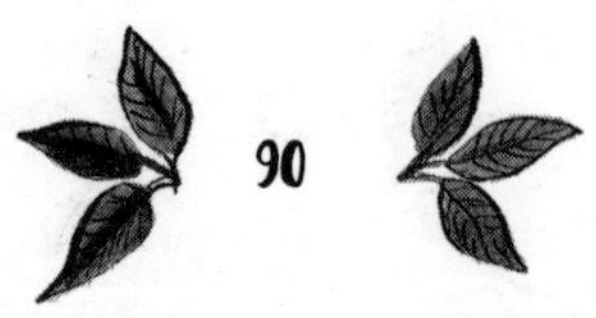

spotted the bird house and all the people still hiding up trees. I could see the tiger keeper hiding in a ditch within the elephant enclosure. Then I saw Oscar coming out from the toilet. He looked up at me and I growled once again. Then I called out, "The tiger has escaped!"

Chapter 14

I circled above the zoo before heading for the town. For the first time, I saw streets and houses. Huge houses next to narrow streets where cars drove slowly close together in a blue smelly cloud.

At last, I found a small green space where four trees and a few bushes grew. I landed on a tree branch there to have a little rest. I

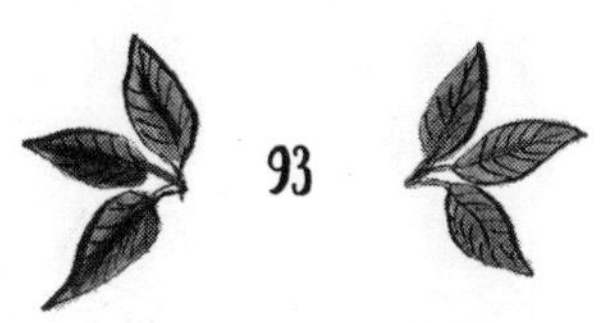

wasn't used to flying after being in captivity for so long.

Sitting below my tree were a pair of sparrows pecking up crumbs from the ground.

"Hi, friends," I called. "I am hungry. Could you spare me a few crumbs?"

"A crow," they spluttered. "Watch out, a crow!" And they scattered away in different directions. Clearly, crows were not very well liked in England.

I ate a few crumbs that were left lying around but they were stale and smelled bad. I flew further until I came across a large park. On the grass I saw a crowd of crows. *Friends at last*, I thought.

"Hello, friends," I called. "Can you help

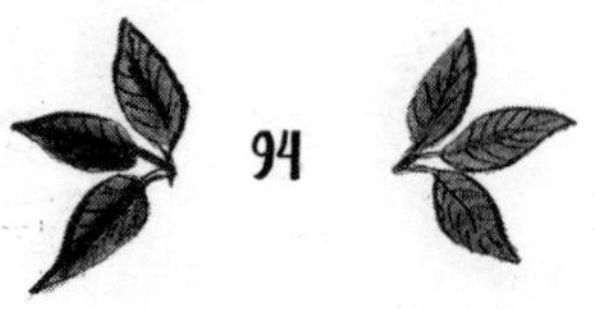

me? I've just escaped from the zoo and I am hungry."

The crows hopped over and looked me up and down.

"What a funny-looking bird," they cackled.

"That's not a crow," croaked another crow.

"It dresses like a crow," said another doubtfully. "But it's clearly *not* a crow."

"It's *pretending* to be a crow!" one of them said scornfully. "Who are you?" she asked me.

"I'm a myna bird," I said proudly.

"Aha, a spy," said the crow. "I told you he wasn't one of us. He's only here to spy on our eating place. Get lost, imposter!" And she flapped towards me, trying to peck me

with her beak.

I flew away as quickly as I could and sat by myself on a branch. Homesickness rolled over me in a wave. I was lonely and sad. I didn't fit in anywhere – I was too much of a crow for other birds to like me, and I wasn't enough of a crow for the real crows!

I was so hungry that I didn't have time to be sad. I even tried nibbling a bit of grass. Yuck! It tasted terrible.

I was trying to swallow a clump of grass when I heard a growl from behind me and

SNAP! I flapped into the air as a sharp set of teeth snatched at the empty space where I had been standing. I threw myself into a tree and perched on a branch, trembling in fear.

Under the tree crouched a dog, barking and jumping. I watched helplessly as more and more dogs joined him. Soon a whole group stood snarling under the tree where I hid.

At last a man and woman strolled past, and whistled to the dogs. The pack of dogs followed them – until they spotted a crow

on the lawn and ran towards it.

"Be careful!" I shouted to the crow. The crow looked up – but there was no time for it to hide. The dogs pounded towards it without stopping. Thinking quickly, I took a deep breath and then roared like the tiger Pandit as loudly as I could: *GRRRRRRRR*.

The dogs stopped in confusion. I growled again and watched in delight as the dogs promptly ran in all directions. For good measure I added, "Help, the tiger has escaped!"

The dogs had gone; the man and woman had gone too. The lawn was suddenly empty and it was quite still. I could hear only the song of a blackbird and the ripple of a brook and, in the far distance, the sound of traffic.

Chapter 15

I flew over to the crow.

"Are you hurt?" I asked.

"No," he answered. "But it was a close shave. Those dogs would have caught me if it weren't for you. So, thank you." He hopped towards me. "My name is Alfred and I'm a raven."

A raven! I thought. Not a crow at all.

"My name is Froggy," I said, "and I am a myna bird."

"Then you are very rare, just like me."

"Here I am," I answered. "But where I'm from, in India, and in Sri Lanka, there are lots of mynas. What about you?"

"There's not many like me around in England," said Alfred. "Ravens are as good as extinct."

"And to think that I thought you were a crow," I said.

Alfred laughed. "They all think that. I thought you were a crow too."

"They all think that," I said, and we both laughed.

"Two rare birds disguised as crows," said Alfred. "What a pair of misfits." He smiled

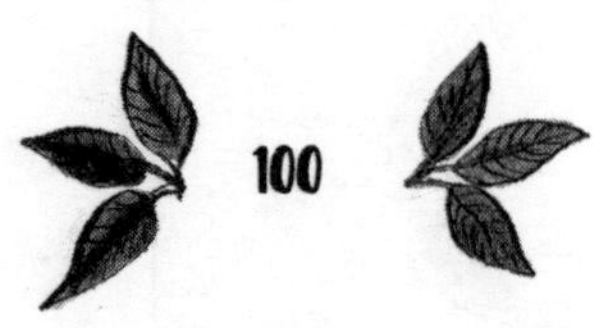

at me and I felt warmer than I had since leaving India.

"I used to live in a small wood near Epping Forest," Alfred explained. "I've only been here in town for three weeks."

"Why did you leave your forest?" I asked.

"That's a long and complicated story," said Alfred with a sigh. "Pesticides."

"What are they?" I wondered aloud.

"Pesticides," Alfred explained, "are chemicals people use to get rid of bugs or mice that eat their crops. It's a poison. So when a mouse eats the corn it's also eating poison – and when we ravens eat the mice, we eat the poison too. I saw too many of my friends get sick so I decided to move to town. Here it's easier to find food that hasn't

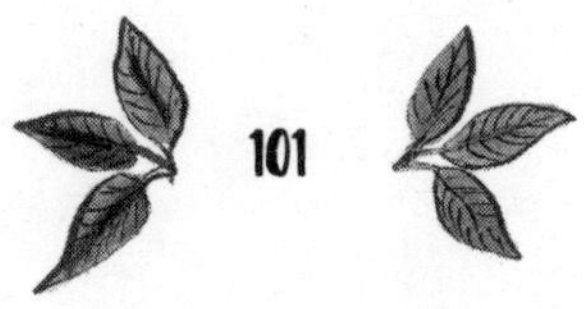

been poisoned."

"Really?" I asked. "I haven't had much luck – and I'm as hungry as a tiger."

Alfred laughed. "Follow me," he said, winging his way into the sky.

Chapter 16

I followed Alfred out of the centre of the city to the city's outskirts. Here there were fewer houses, broken up by green fields and small woods. In a meadow between three large trees stood a house. To one side, a bird house had been placed on a pole. In front of the house was a wooden board and corn, slices of apple and pieces of meat. My

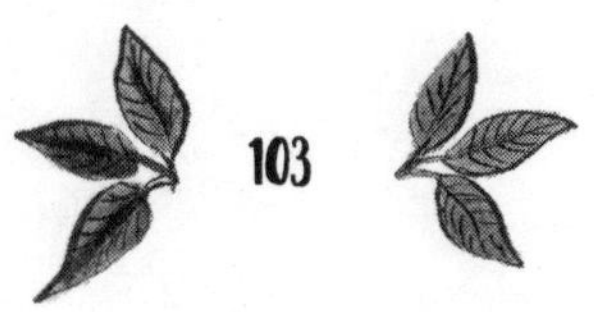

tummy rumbled.

We perched on a branch. I noticed that there was a man down there too.

"The table has been well laid," said Alfred.

I looked down and thought of the man who had captured us in the jungle. "It's not a trap, is it? Does that man want to catch us?"

"No," said Alfred, "you don't have to be afraid. Here you can eat in peace. The man won't harm you – he's an ornithologist."

"Ornitho-what?" I asked.

"Or-ni-tho-lo-gist," said Alfred. "A scientist who observes birds. This one just does it for fun. He puts the food out hoping we'll come and visit."

I turned around and looked at the man. He was crouching behind a bush and

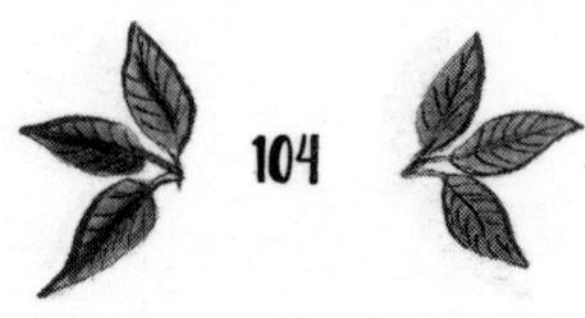

watching the table through binoculars.

"Don't stare at him," said Alfred. "Pretend you don't know he's there."

I soon forgot the birdwatcher, as I tucked in to the feast. I ate and ate until I was stuffed! When I simply couldn't manage another mouthful, I belched and let out a contented coo like a pigeon. The man dropped his binoculars in amazement.

"A crow with a yellow stripe on its head that belches and coos like a pigeon – there's no such thing," he shouted, and quickly ran indoors. He came out holding a large book and began turning the pages. In the book were pictures of numerous birds.

"Good job," said Alfred. "One of the happiest moments for an ornithologist is

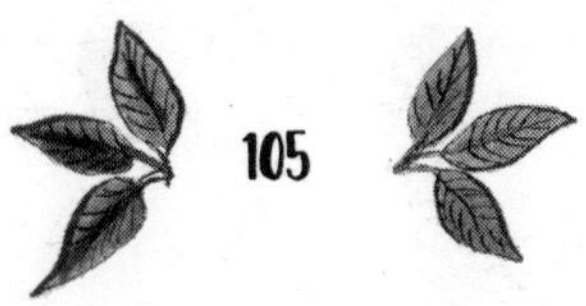

when they believe they've just discovered a new species of bird. We'll be able to come back tomorrow!"

Chapter 17

Alfred asked me where I would l prefer to live. He said there were loads of different options – I could have a nest on the ground, among the reeds, up in a tree or in the mud.

"At home in the jungle, we live in a hollow in a tree."

"Then I have just the thing for you," said Alfred.

We flew to an old oak tree that had clearly been struck by lightning. It was blackened and half-destroyed, but the trunk had many hollows. It was perfect.

Alfred built a higgledy-piggledy nest in the treetop for himself and I settled into a cosy hollow in the oak. From my warm nest I had a good view of a meadow where I could watch the cows munching the grass.

All through the night I could hear the sound of munching and it soothed me to sleep. It was wonderful here. When it rained, I was protected, and when the sun was hot and scorching, I sat in the shade. All our food was provided by the ornithologist and he photographed me and taped my cooing on a tape recorder.

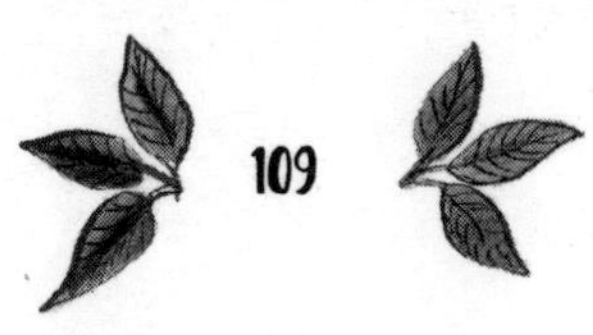

"Let him have his fun," said Alfred.

And so, the days and weeks went by. Everything was perfect – until the cold weather began.

The green leaves lost their colour and slowly changed to yellow, brown and red. I sat in my tree hollow and shivered so much my beak started to chatter.

"It's so c-c-cold," I said to Alfred. "In the jungle it's always warm."

"It will only get colder," said Alfred, frowning. "And the water will turn to ice."

"What is ice?" I asked.

"Ice is made when it gets so cold that the water freezes – that means it goes hard. Then when it snows the ground is covered in white." Alfred looked at me doubtfully.

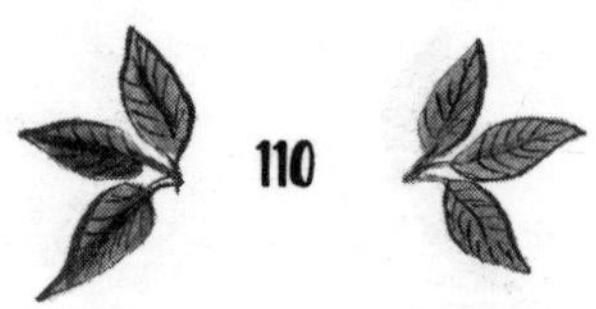

"I don't think you're meant to be outside in the winter. We must find somewhere for you to stay when it gets really cold. Do you know anyone who would take you in?"

"No," I said sadly. "Not really. Except for a little girl … but her mother doesn't want me. And, anyway, I don't know where she lives."

"I will think of something," promised Alfred.

On that same night came the first frost. It crept slowly up the tree trunk into my hollow and through the leaves which I had nestled in. I was too cold to move. When Alfred came to visit me, I was sitting stiff and motionless.

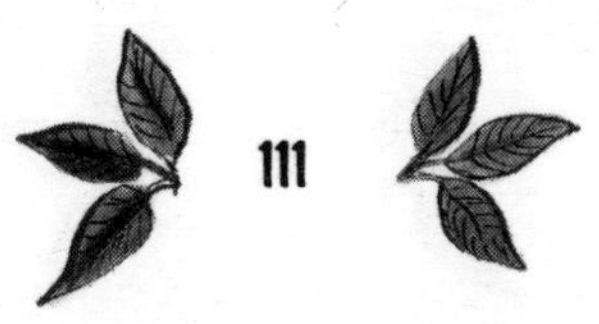

"Froggy!" he gasped. Pulling me on to his back, he flapped his powerful wings and flew away with me. Although Alfred was big and strong, he was out of breath and breathing heavily when he reached the next house. There, he laid me on the windowsill and tapped loudly on the glass with his beak. He waited until someone came to the door and then flew away.

A man and a boy came out of the house to see what all the noise was about.

"Look there," said the boy, pointing at the window. "There's a bird. A special sort of bird."

The father looked at me suspiciously. "It doesn't look very special to me. Just an ordinary crow."

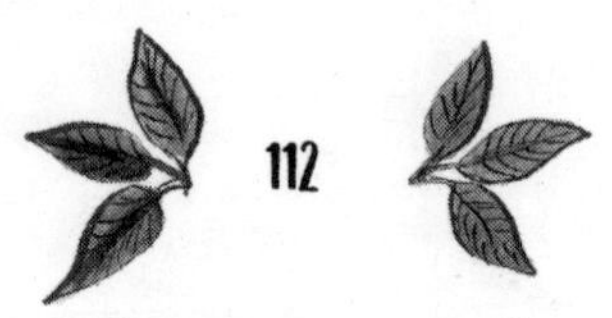

"That is not a crow," said the boy firmly. "Anyway, he's frozen. Can we bring him into the house to warm him? Please?"

"That's all I need," said his dad. "You bringing a frozen crow into the house!"

I tried to sing like a nightingale to show the man that I was not a crow, but I was so frozen that I could only manage a raspy, "*CAW CAW*."

"I told you," said his dad. "A common crow. Leave it where it is. They're full of germs."

He pulled the boy into the house and closed the door.

A moment later, the boy snuck out of the house wearing a coat and holding a basket lined with paper. He gently laid me inside.

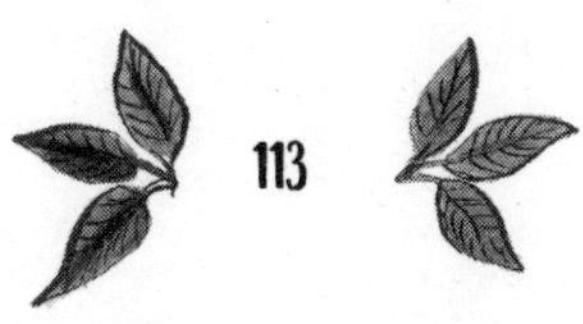

He picked up the basket, climbed on to his bike, and cycled off.

Chapter 18

When he stopped, we were standing outside somewhere I recognized. It was Mr Lyon's pet shop!

The boy carried me inside. I saw Mr Lyon's large hands reaching into the basket and then he picked me up.

"Ah!" said Mr Lyon. "A myna. I know this one." And his big ears began to glow

with excitement.

He placed me in a cage and propped it next to a heater. "Thanks for bringing him in. He'll thaw out there," he said, and gave the boy a couple of coins. "Go and buy yourself an ice cream," he said, shooing the boy – who was craning his neck to see the animals – out into the freezing cold.

Mr Lyon grinned at me. "So. You've come back to me at just the right time. There is someone who is interested in you – an animal impersonator! Three days ago his talking parrot got eaten by a cat."

Despite the warmth of the heater, I felt a chill rush through me. For a moment, I had hoped that Mr Lyon would return me

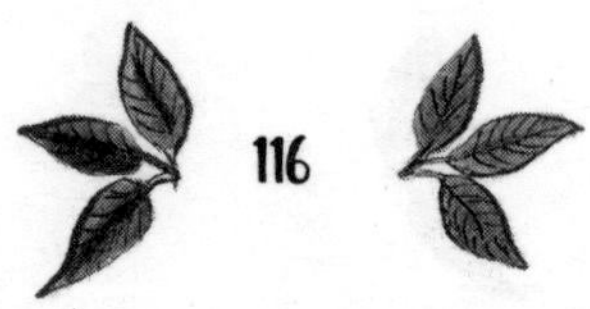

to the zoo and that I might be reunited with Blackbeard. I closed my eyes in despair, drifting off into an uneasy sleep.

The next day, the animal impersonator arrived.

"There he is," said Mr Lyon, and pointed at me.

The animal impersonator came over to my cage, leaning on his walking stick.

"Yes, yes," he said, "a myna bird, perfect. The mynas may not look interesting, but they are very clever."

Then, to my surprise, he spoke to me in my own myna language. "If you'll work with me, you'll be well fed, warm and be given a large cage."

My beak gaped open – I had never

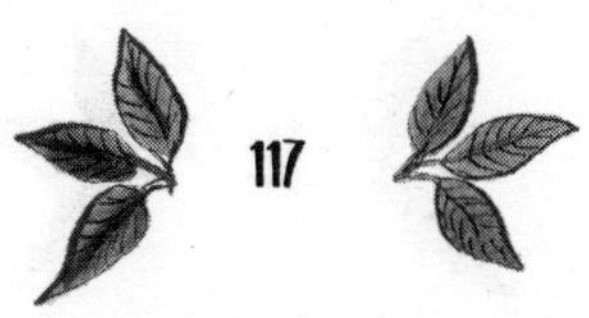

met a human who could speak the myna language.

"And what must I do?" I asked suspiciously.

"It's very simple: you must talk like a human. We'll perform together."

"I can do that," I said.

The animal impersonator handed three notes to Jug-Ears and we left. It turned out that I was only worth a few little bits of paper.

Chapter 19

I soon learned that the impersonator was called Mr Clever. He brought me to his house on the riverbank that he shared with a large black cat named Alexander. When Alexander yawned I could see every one of his huge, pointed teeth. I couldn't help but shudder with fear when he came near, remembering what had happened to

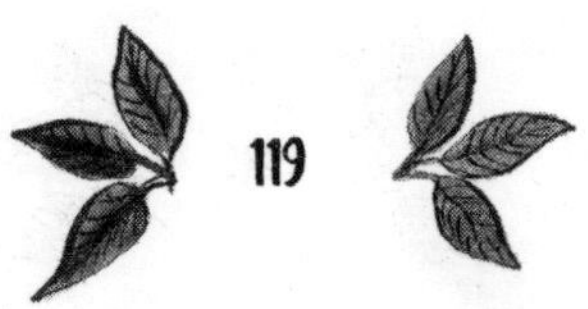

Mr Clever's talking parrot.

I found out that Alexander was not only big and dangerously quick, but he was also smart. He had figured out how to open the small door to the birdcage, which was how he had got to the talking parrot. "Watch out for Alexander," Mr Clever told me. "I've put a safety lock on the birdcage after last time – but he's very sneaky."

Mr Clever turned out to be as clever as his name. He could imitate every animal sound and talk to all of us, including a tortoise. You could see the animal impersonator's lips move and, after a while, the tortoise would slowly turn its head towards him and move its mouth.

My cage was in a room with a view of

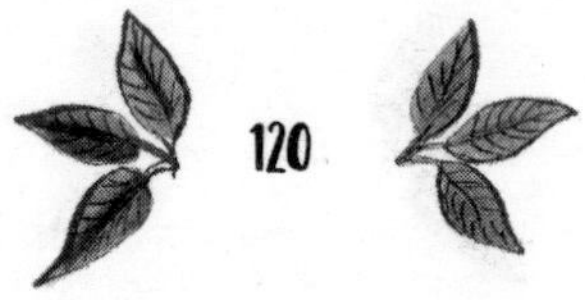

the canal. I watched the boats sailing slowly by and thought of the ship that brought me to England. These boats were long and small, not as high and wide as the ship I had travelled on. I dreamed of being on one of the narrow boats, seeing the countryside as I travelled, flying above from time to time to see the trees and mountains.

Once I was settled, the animal impersonator told me it was time to start work. "We've got one week before we're appearing on a children's TV programme," he said. "The idea is that we'll swap – you be the human and I'll be all the animals. So, let's practise! Repeat after me: 'Good dog. Come to heel.'"

I repeated, "Come, Jasper, heel."

Mr Clever yapped like a dog, whimpered, howled a little and then spoke in his usual voice: "Good. Now say 'nice horsey'."

Mr Clever neighed like a brewery carthorse. As we practised, he grunted, bleated, miaowed and I named the animals in English. It all came easily to me, and Mr Clever was delighted.

We practised every morning and in the afternoon I sat alone in the room and watched the river, dreaming of flying outside above the boats.

By now, the trees had lost their leaves and stood quite bare. I thought sadly of the trees at home which were green all year round. The only good thing about the bare trees in my new home was that I could see

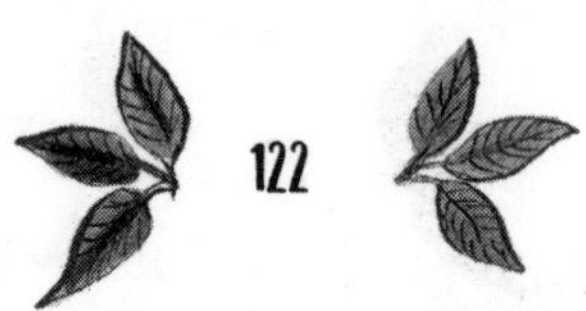

through the branches and look at all the boats sailing by.

One day, I saw a red boat winding its way past my window. On the boat, I saw a girl I recognized riding her bike around the deck. It was the girl that I knew from the pet shop, the one who had nicknamed me the pirate blackbird. It was a name that I liked very much – so much better than boring old myna. I shouted *"hello"* but because of the distance the girl couldn't hear me through the window.

The boat passed slowly by and vanished around the river bend.

"Who are you talking to?" asked Alexander. He had come in so quietly I hadn't even seen him there. He was able

to open doors by leaping on to the handles and pushing them down.

"No one," I said. "I was trying to speak to a girl I met before. She was on one of those boats."

Alexander purred disinterestedly. He eyed me in his cage. "Are you bored? I am *terribly* bored. There aren't any other animals here to play with. Not even a mouse or a dog. Not that I like dogs." He gave a shudder. "But it would be a bit more exciting. Unless … *you* wanted to play with me? Maybe a game of catch?"

Now, in the jungle we didn't have any cats, but I was used to dealing with tigers. I knew Alexander was up to something.

"No thanks," I said. "Not in the mood

for catch."

"Hmm," murmured Alexander. "What about flying round the house a bit?"

"No thanks," I answered quickly. "I'm very happy here in my cage, thank you. And, besides, I've forgotten how to fly."

"Okay," said Alexander. "That's fine by me. But why don't I try to open your cage, just for a bit of fun."

"Keep your paws away from my cage," I squawked.

Alexander ignored me. He jumped at the lock and managed to turn it. I began to scream at the top of my voice.

At that moment, Mr Clever burst into the room. He saw Alexander by the cage door, and roared, "Don't you even think

about eating another of my birds! Get out!" And he chased Alexander out of the room. He came back to check on me. "Don't worry," he said reassuringly. "In future I will lock the door so that he can't come into the room."

Chapter 20

The day finally arrived when Mr Clever and I were to make our first appearance on kids' TV. I was brought to the television studio in my cage. Mr Clever carried me into a room with many glaring lights. Three large black boxes were set up with people sitting down behind them.

"The cameras," whispered Mr Clever.

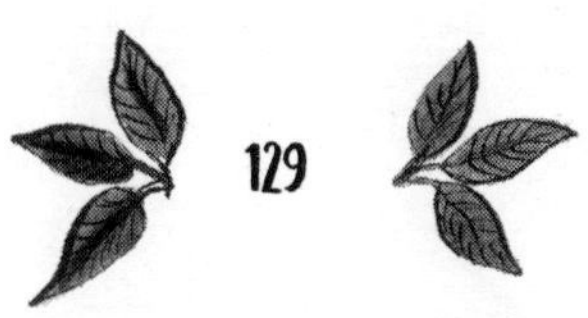

"Soon our pictures will be chopped into many little dots, fired through these cables and finally they'll arrive on the TV screens at home where all the little dots get re-assembled."

It sounded awful. "No way," I said fearfully. "I am not taking part."

"Don't worry," said Mr Clever, "it doesn't hurt. It's all down to electronics."

As my eyes became accustomed to the glaring lights, I could see a crowd of children sitting in the room. A woman with a fixed smile on her face introduced the programme.

Someone shouted: "Attention, we are on air."

"Good luck," whispered Mr Clever.

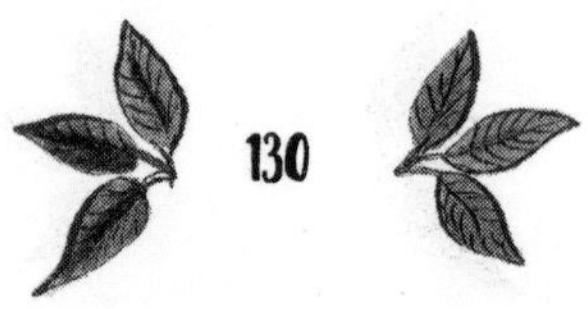

The woman spoke: "Hello, dear children here in our studio and at home! Today we have an animal impersonator as our guest – he can pretend to be any animal you can think of! Welcome, Mr Clever."

The children all clapped and cheered. In answer, Mr Clever made a sound like a rooster: *Cock-a-doodle-doo.*

"Now, tell me, Mr Clever – is that a crow?" asked the woman, pointing at me (very rudely, I thought).

"Pointing is rude," I told her.

The smile disappeared from the woman's face and the children burst into laughter.

I remembered what we were there for. "Nice doggie," I said.

Mr Clever barked like a dog. We

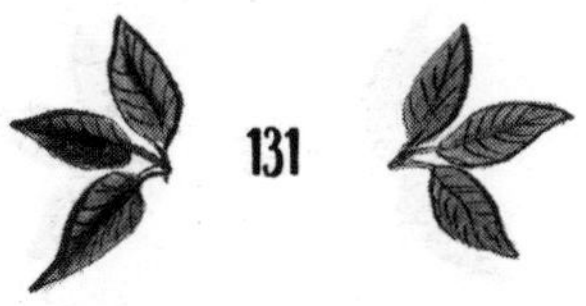

continued our act impersonating all the animal and human sounds.

To round up the act, I shouted, "Help, the tiger has escaped." The animal impersonator roared like a tiger. His roar was not the sound of a real tiger in the jungle but that of a tamer, older, timid zoo tiger. *Not good enough*, I thought. One last time, I roared just like Pandit at home in the jungle. The children screamed, the woman dropped her microphone and the camera operators jumped in shock from their cameras and ran out of the studio.

The TV screens went blank.

Chapter 21

When we were back home, Mr Clever had a stern chat with me. "All your impressions were good, but you must only say the things we have practised," he told me. "Because this week we're going on tour."

A tour turned out to mean travelling through many towns and villages doing our act. I was excited at the thought of

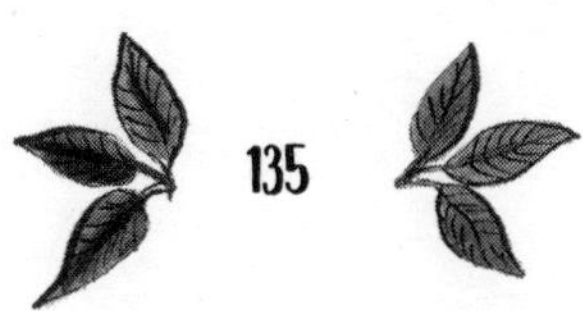

seeing lots of new places. But we never saw the towns themselves – instead, all we saw was the inside of classrooms, sports clubs and care homes.

At night we travelled by train. I sat in a small travel cage. Mr Clever slept in his seat and snored loudly. Unlike me, he missed Alexander the cat very much. Each day was much the same – we rode by taxi to our performances, performed and then returned by train.

The winter slowly passed and spring arrived. Outside my window, the birds began to sing and the trees which had been bare for so long turned green. I longed to be able to fly freely again, but Mr Clever didn't let me out of the house in case I escaped.

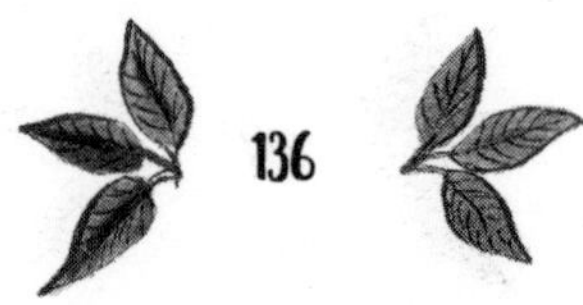

When we were not travelling, I sat in my cage and looked at the river. Now and then I would see the little red ship passing by – the home of the little girl from the pet shop. I began wondering whether I could escape from my cage.

During a show for firefighters, I was thinking so hard that I forgot to perform at all! I simply sat speechless. Mr Clever was forced to act out the number alone. He spoke and mimicked the animal sounds until he became hoarse. He roared like a tiger but it sounded like the creaking of a rusty door. The audience laughed and heckled and at the end of the show some people demanded their money back. After all, they had paid to see a talking bird, not a silent one.

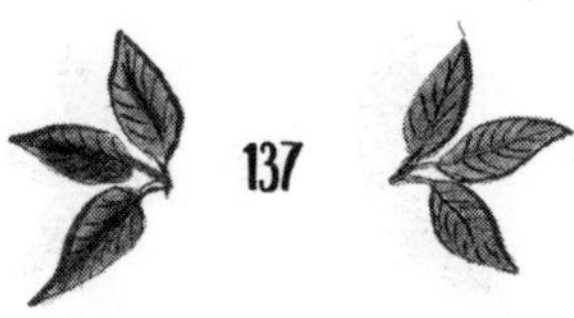

"It's just a crow," shouted one particularly loud man, pointing at me. "He can't speak a word."

"He can speak," croaked Mr Clever, tired from all his efforts. "But today he's ill."

At home, Mr Clever placed me in the cage. "You spoilt the whole show! We had a deal. If you won't speak then you don't get anything to eat. Understood?"

Chapter 22

I had to get out of the cage and escape. But how? The safety lock could only be opened by Mr Clever or Alexander.

Which gave me an idea.

The next day, I asked Mr Clever to place me on the patio.

"Please! I just need some fresh air. Then I'm sure I'll be able to talk again," I said.

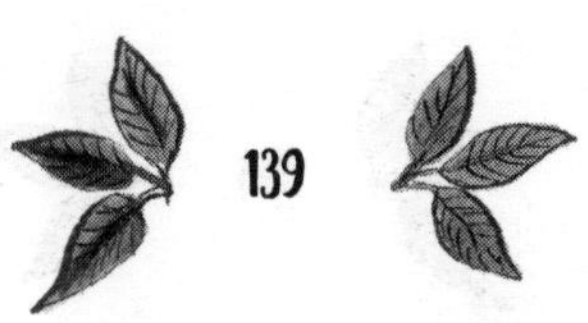

Mr Clever carried me out, grumbling under his breath.

He went back into the house. A little later, Alexander appeared. He lay on the wall and stared at me. I stared back. I needed to ask for help from one of my friends. But who? Blackbeard was stuck in the zoo, and Alfred was miles away.

Unless … Alfred wasn't here, but there were other birds who could help me get a message to him!

A sparrow was pecking at crumbs on the ground a little way off, and I called out to her. "Please help me! Can you fly as quickly as you can to Alfred the raven? His nest is in an oak tree on the edge of town. Tell him to come here as quickly as he can."

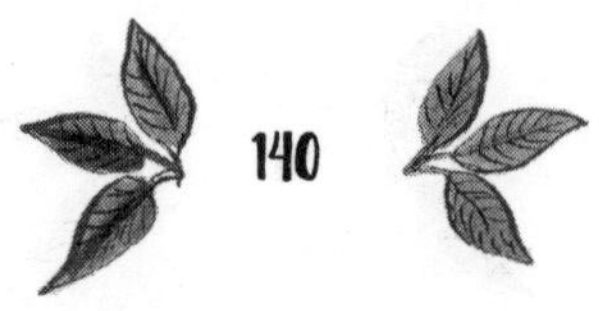

The sparrow was happy to help and I gave her directions. After she flew off, I sat in my cage and waited, nervously watching Alexander licking his lips beneath my cage. Suddenly, he stood up and came a few steps nearer, lay down again and stared at me. Very slowly, he tapped the ground with the tip of his tail. I knew he was about to pounce.

Just as I was giving up hope, Alfred arrived.

"Alfred," I shouted, "I am here in the cage."

"Hello, my famous friend," called Alfred, "Good to see you! I've heard about your amazing act! I want to hear all about it!"

"I will tell you everything!" I promised.

"But first I need your help. I'm trapped in this cage and the cat wants to eat me. Please get me out of here!"

"Sure," said Alfred. "But how?"

I thought fast. I remembered Alexander saying that he didn't like dogs. "Try to bark," I said.

Alfred barked – but it sounded like a hoarse pig grunting.

"That was good, wasn't it?" asked Alfred proudly.

"Yes," I said doubtfully, watching Alexander the cat, who lay watching me, unblinking. I knew I could do a brilliant bark – but unfortunately so did Alexander, who had seen me perform my act a hundred times. "Could you try and make it sound a

bit more realistic?" I asked.

"I thought it sounded very realistic," said Alfred, looking put out.

"Well, okay," I said, "but the cat over there doesn't think so."

"Just listen," said Alfred, and tried once again to bark.

Alexander blinked his eyes and yawned in boredom.

"It's not enough," I said. "There's only one thing for it. You must fly to the zoo and get Blackbeard the parrot."

"Isn't he in a cage?"

"He's just going to have to get out of it. Otherwise that cat over there is going to eat me."

Quickly, Alfred flew away. I sat in my

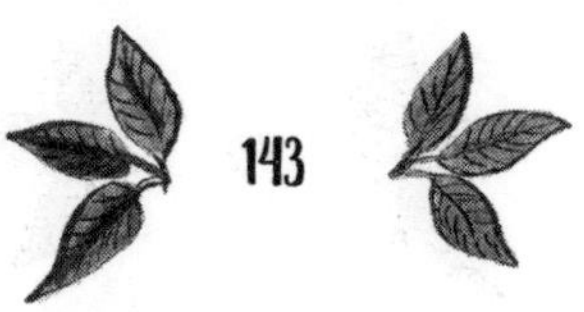

cage and waited. *Hopefully Blackbeard can escape*, I thought. *Hopefully he can still fly. Hopefully he can get here fast enough…*

Alexander stood up and crept around my cage. He miaowed, stretched and showed me his big sharp claws.

"Wouldn't you like to come out of the cage for a bit?" asked Alexander. "We could play hide-and-seek."

"No thank you," I said. "I'm tired. A bit under the weather."

"How about I visit you in your cage?"

"Then I will shout for Mr Clever," I said. "And he won't be pleased with you."

"It was only a joke," growled Alexander. "Have it your way."

He lay down in front of the cage door

and waited. He probably hoped I would fall asleep.

Slowly it grew dark, and my fear grew. Then I saw something – Alfred, flapping through the dusk. And behind him was Blackbeard!

"Blackbeard," I shouted. "At last!"

"Urgh," gasped Blackbeard, totally out of breath. He sat on the roof. "What are you doing, besides sitting around in your posh cage next to that horrible cat?"

"It's a long story. How did you manage to escape from the zoo?"

"Ahh, that was a piece of cake," said Blackbeard. "I simply shouted *FIRE*. Then Oscar – who really is a good chap – quickly opened all the doors of the birdcages. He

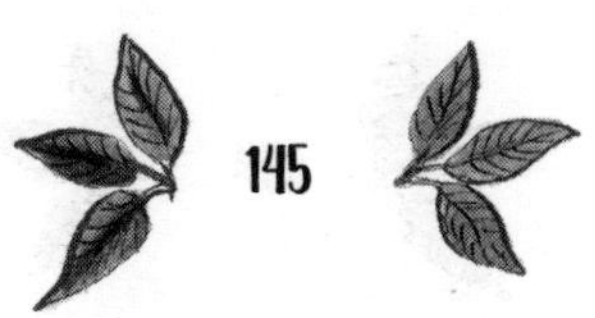

didn't want any of the birds to get burnt. He shouldn't get into trouble – none of the other birds flew away. But I did. So, tell me, what's the problem here?"

"I want to escape," I said.

"Again?" said Blackbeard. "How are you going to do that?"

"I've got a plan," I said, "but I need to whisper it to you because of that monster cat."

Blackbeard sat on my cage and Alexander immediately stood up.

"Make it quick," said Blackbeard.

"The cat can open the door," I whispered. "So my plan is, I let him."

"Okay," said Blackbeard, "but then he'll eat you."

"Exactly!" I said. "And I don't want that.

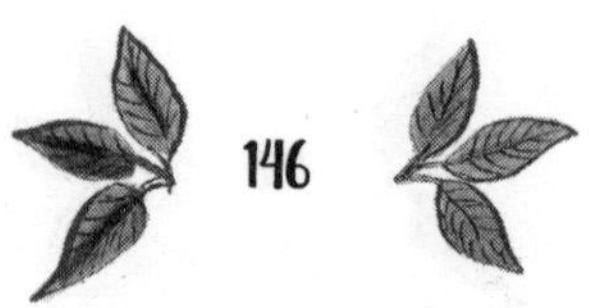

So in that moment when he opens the cage door you must bark really wildly like a dog, right behind him. If this cat is scared of anything, it's dogs."

"I'll do it," said Blackbeard. "I just hope I can pull this off."

"Be careful!" I called.

Alexander had already crept closer and looked ready to pounce on Blackbeard, who flew quickly high up to join Alfred on the roof of the house.

I took a deep breath. It was time to escape.

Chapter 23

I was afraid. Of course I was. One wrong step and Alexander would have his claws in me. I took one more deep breath and then called out, “Alexander! Come over here, will you?”

Alexander came and stood close to me. Only the wire of the cage separated us.

“Do you see my two friends over there?”

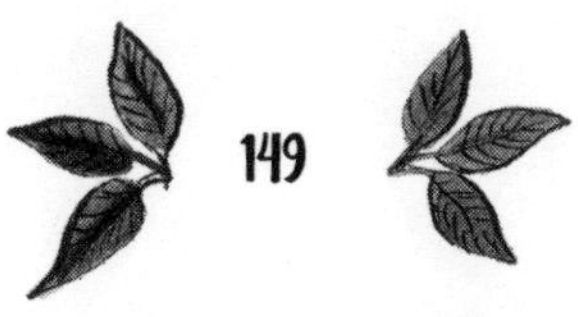

I nodded at the roof where Blackbeard and Alfred were waiting. "I'd love to go and sit with them on the roof, just for a minute. Would you please open the cage door? I'll be back in the cage in no time."

Alexander thought about it for a minute and said, "No."

"Why's that?" I asked.

"When I open your cage door you'll scream that I'm trying to eat you and then Mr Clever will come and I'll be in big trouble. No, mate, you can't fool me."

"Just listen," I said. "First of all, I am not your mate. And second of all, I promise you that I won't scream, if *you* promise not to harm me."

"I gladly promise you that," said

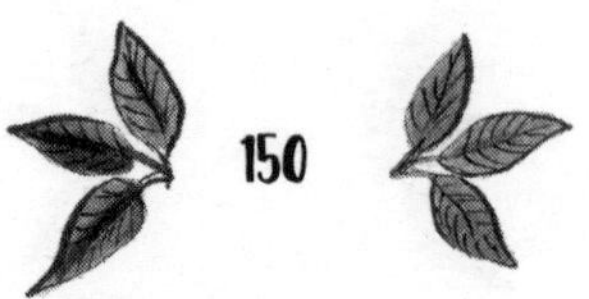

Alexander, and licked his lips.

"Good," I said. "Then open the door, will you?"

Alexander sat on his back legs and deftly pulled the catch away with his front paw. Then he opened the bars with his teeth. The wire door swung open.

"Right," hissed the cat. "Now I'm going to *get you.*"

His front paw was already in the cage, and I saw his big pointed teeth ready to snap down on my neck. But, at exactly that moment, we heard the bark of a furious dog.

Blackbeard had done it.

With one leap Alexander hurled himself inside the cage, shaking with fright. As he pressed against the bars, I shot out of the cage.

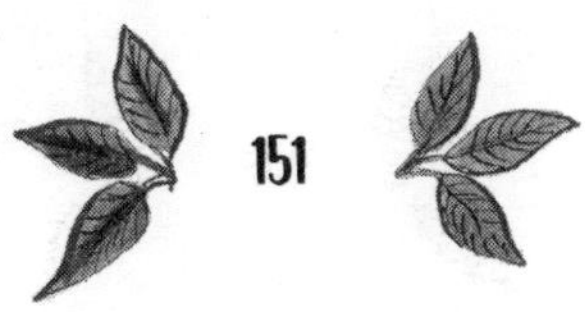

I was free! I quickly shoved the door closed behind me and with a click it was locked.

There sat the big dangerous cat, trapped in my cage. Blackbeard and Alfred laughed so much they nearly fell off the roof.

Alexander raged and spat at us.

"Just you wait till I get out! You'll be sorry."

I smiled slyly at him, and then I opened my beak and cried, "Help! Help!"

Mr Clever sprinted out of the house and over to the cage. Alexander tried to make himself as small as possible in the cage. Mr Clever made his way to the cage. He peered in and then began to splutter: "The myna bird is gone! My precious myna! You naughty cat, have you eaten

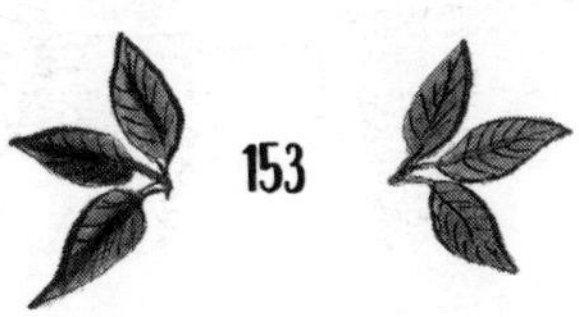

the myna? The most gifted bird in the world. Why, I – I – I'm going to sell you to the pet shop!"

Mr Clever was in such a rage, I thought he was going to do it. This had gone too far.

I called out, "Good doggie!"

Mr Clever stopped and stared into the trees until he spotted me. "My myna," he called, "lovely bird. My colleague! My partner! Please come back. I'll feed you as much as you can eat. Please come back." He started to make clucking noises, waving me down from the tree.

"Has he lost the plot?" asked Blackbeard. "He thinks you are a chicken."

"Yes," I said, "the poor man is a little mixed up."

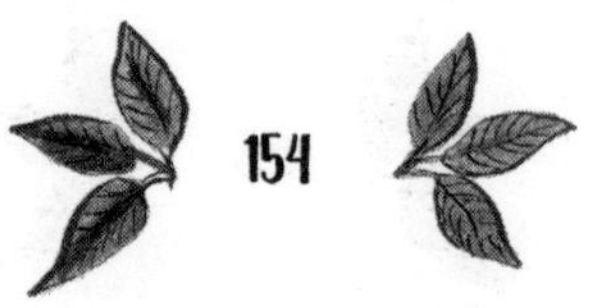

Mr Clever had started to neigh like a horse now.

"He's completely lost it," said Blackbeard.

But I couldn't worry about Mr Clever, not when I was free at last! I stretched my wings, calling out, "Hip hip hooray!"

Then, I flew high up into the air. It was wonderful to feel the air rushing through my wings, to finally be able to fly. Blackbeard and Alfred joined me, and together we flew over the countryside. The people standing below looked up and stared wherever we went. We were a strange motley bunch: one bird who roared like a tiger, one who grunted like a hoarse pig and one, flying a little behind, singing:

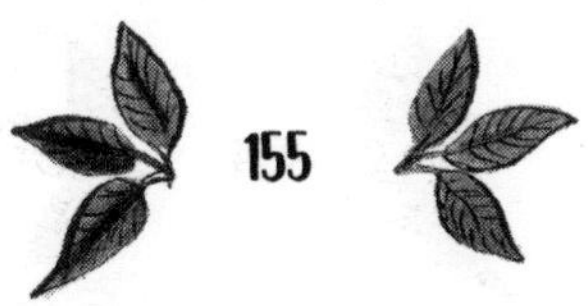

"Oh I'd like to be on a ship at sea
Only the crew, the captain and me.
Steady hand on the helm
And a small rum tot,
gentle wind, calm sea…
We're pleased with our lot!"

Chapter 24

We flew quite a distance until Blackbeard started to lag behind.

"Slow down, boys," he called. "I can't keep up with you youngsters."

We sat down on a beech tree by the riverbank and Blackbeard caught his breath.

"What are you going to do now?" Alfred asked me.

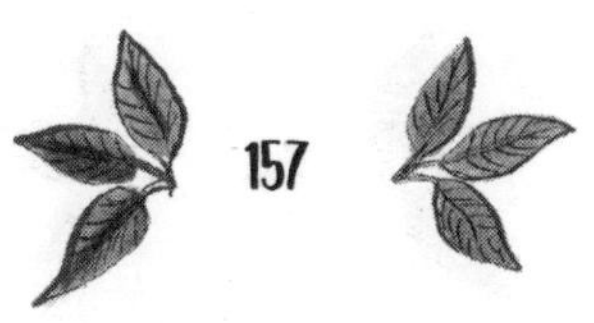

I was too happy to worry. "I'm just going to fly around," I said. "It's wonderful being out here in the open."

"Yes, it is in summer," said Blackbeard. "But in winter you have to have a roof over your head otherwise you'll freeze."

"I know," I replied, remembering how cold I had been in the winter. "But I can't go back into a cage again. I have to be free to fly."

"Better you than me," said Blackbeard. "That journey was quite lovely, a real adventure. But at my age the zoo is the best place to be. Even if Matilda and William, those squabbling birds of paradise, get on my nerves."

"What are *you* going to do?" I asked Alfred.

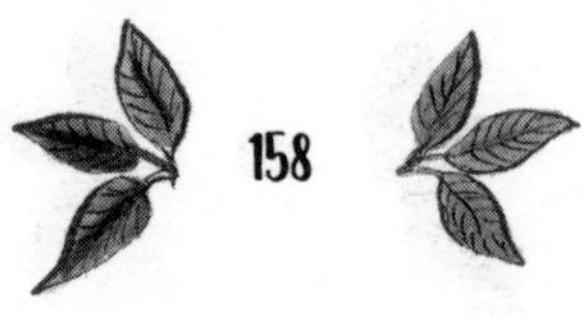

"My wood is too noisy. All day long you hear the screeching of tyres. I think it's time to go back to my oak tree near the ornithologist again. He had the best food."

"Couldn't the three of us just fly around the country together?" I asked pleadingly.

"Sorry," said Blackbeard. "I'm too old for that."

I looked away, heartbroken to think that I would be by myself again. And there in the distance I saw a familiar red boat approaching the river bend. My eyes lit up.

"What if we travelled by boat?" I asked.

"By boat?" said Blackbeard.

"By river boat, to be specific," I said, pointing down at the little red narrow boat.

"Well, knock me down with a feather, a

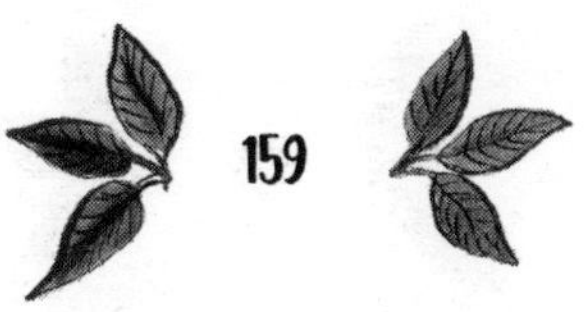

river boat," said Blackbeard. "But I travelled on a sailing ship, not a puny little river boat. My ship had as many masts as a forest has trees. That little boat won't be half as good."

"Look, it travels on water and also has an anchor," I said firmly. "You can sit there and view the scenery and hear the swish of the water."

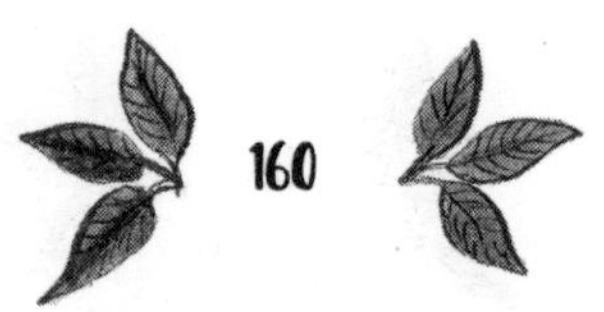

Blackbeard thought for a moment. "Oh, maybe you're right. I would love to let the wind blow over my beak once more…"

"Come on then," I said. "Let's go introduce ourselves."

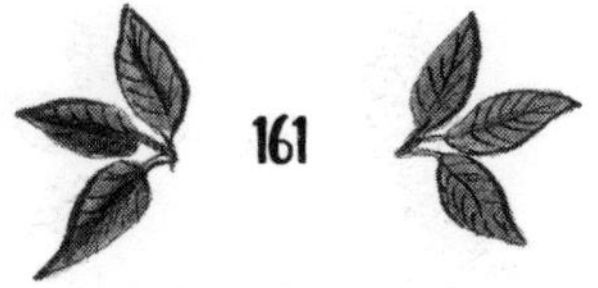

Chapter 25

We flew over to the boat and sat on the railing of the bridge. Behind the helm stood a woman. I recognized her as the little girl's mother.

"It's a bit small," said Blackbeard, looking around. "And it doesn't have any masts. At least it has a cabin and a navigation bridge ... but a woman at the helm, that's outrageous!

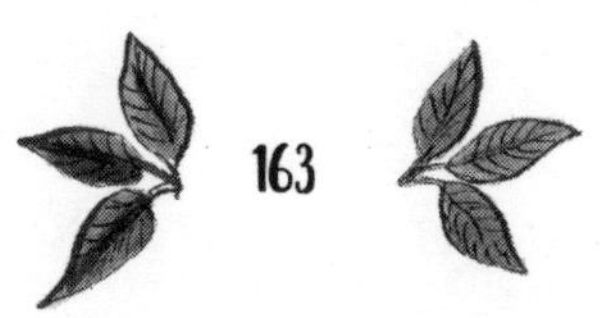

What kind of a captain is that who allows such a thing? That isn't a boat for me."

I sighed. Blackbeard was very old-fashioned and it had been a very, very long time since he had been on a boat.

The woman at the helm whistled with two fingers and a sailor appeared. She said, "Scare those three birds away, will you, Harry? They'll poo over everything."

Harry was just about to scare us away with the end of a rope when he was interrupted by a little girl coming out of the cabin, calling: "Mummy, that's the pirate blackbird!"

"Nonsense," said her mother. "That's just a crow. Two crows and an ancient old parrot. Harry, get rid of them, will you?"

"Yes, captain," he answered.

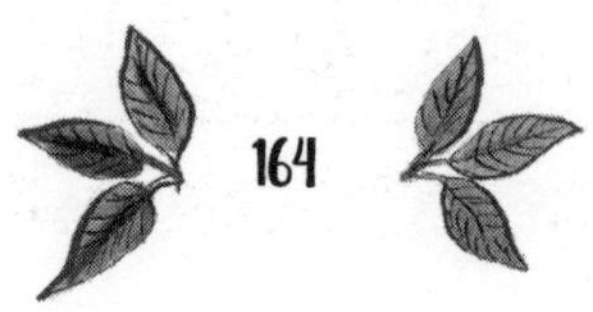

"What's this?" cried Blackbeard. "That woman is the captain?"

I sighed again.

Harry approached us, holding the end of the rope in his right hand.

"Oh, please, Mummy," said the little girl. "I promise you, it's the pirate blackbird."

Harry raised the rope. Quickly, I started to bark like a dog. Harry stood there, rope in his raised hand.

"What on earth?" he cried. "That bird is barking at me!"

The woman stared, flabbergasted, and took her eye off her ship's course. If Blackbeard hadn't suddenly shouted "*Hard a-starboard*", the boat would have hit the bridge pillar.

The captain gave us a thoughtful look.

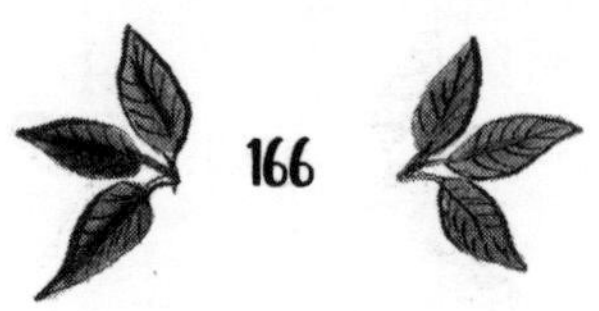

"That parrot is a good sailor," she said. "Maybe they can stay for a bit."

And so we were allowed to remain on board.

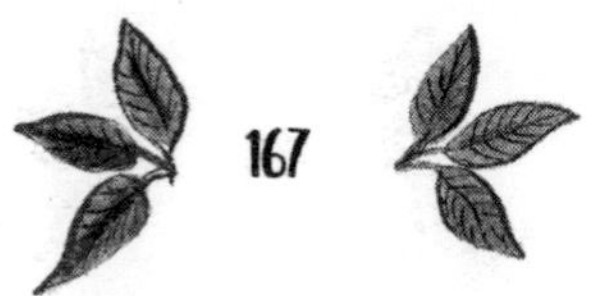

Chapter 26

Alfred, Blackbeard and I have stayed on that river boat ever since.

We have travelled all through England, on the Thames, the Severn, the Avon and sometimes the Mersey. It is wonderful to sit on a boat when it rocks a little and the water ripples and swishes quietly, passing the houses, trees, hills, villages and castles.

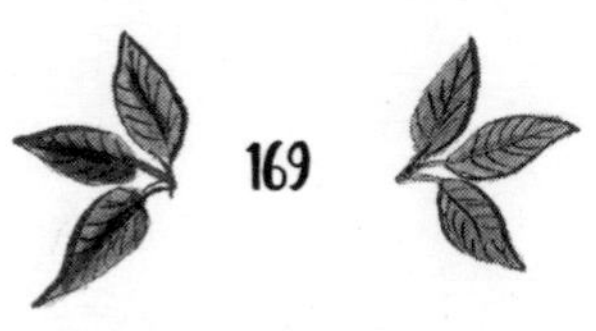

It took a while for Blackbeard to admit that the woman is a very good captain. Maybe the best he's seen in his long years at sea. Now and then, when a strong wind blows and the boat rocks on the river, Blackbeard will sing,

"Oh I'd like to be on a ship at sea,
Only the waves, the captain and me!"

Alfred has built himself a nest in a lifeboat. "Better to be safe than sorry," he says.

I often fly a short distance from the boat and sit on a tree by the riverbank. There I wait until the boat sweeps around the river bend, the red bow sporting a white beard.

In the evenings, the boat docks on the riverbank and Harry throws the anchor overboard. Then Alfred, Blackbeard, the

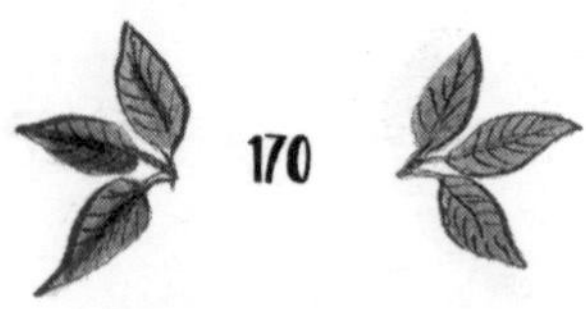

little girl and I will sit in the twilight on deck. Blackbeard recalls the time when he sailed a big sailing ship and roamed the seven seas. He tells us about pirate treasures, enormous waves and sea monsters. Tall tales.

The little girl sits there and listens with inquisitive eyes. When the captain asks: "Why are you hanging around with these birds?" she answers, "I am listening to Blackbeard's stories. He was a pirate too once, you know."

"You have a vivid imagination," says her mother, shaking her head.

"But they really are telling me stories," the girl protests, and her mother walks off, laughing.

"Don't worry about it," Blackbeard says

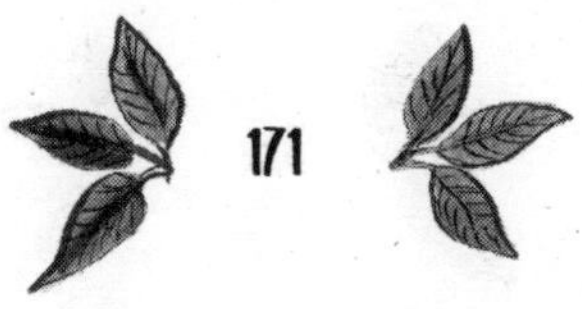

with a grin. "She's not so bad, and she can't help it. After all, she's just one of those grown-uppeties."

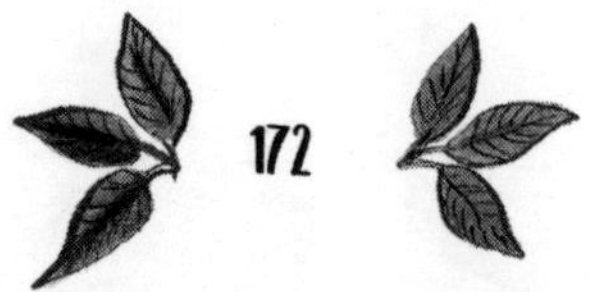